"I…thought you … began, then sipp… had cooled down just enough to be palatable without burning.

"Yes?"

Her teeth pressed into her lip.

"God, this is way harder than it should be," she said on a humorless laugh. If only he knew how much this was her worst nightmare. Not being pregnant, but all the circumstances surrounding it.

"Libby, are you okay?"

"No," she groaned, placing her tea on the bench. "Not really." She frowned. "And yes, at the same time."

"That makes no sense."

"I know," she said softly, sucking in a deep breath. "The thing is…" She stared at her tea rather than into his eyes, which were too perceptive, too inquisitive. Too everything. "The thing is," she started again, "that night…"

Silence fell, except for the ticking of the clock, which sat on the kitchen bench. Strange, she'd never really noticed how imperious and loud it was before. Every second cranked noisily past.

"Raul, I'm pregnant," she said, finally, the words, now she'd committed to saying them, rushing out of her. "Three and a half months pregnant, in fact. You're the father."

Clare Connelly was raised in small-town Australia among a family of avid readers. She spent much of her childhood up a tree, Harlequin book in hand. Clare is married to her own real-life hero, and they live in a bungalow near the sea with their two children. She is frequently found staring into space—a surefire sign she is in the world of her characters. She has a penchant for French food and ice-cold champagne, and Harlequin novels continue to be her favorite-ever books. Writing for Harlequin Presents is a long-held dream. Clare can be contacted via clareconnelly.com or on her Facebook page.

Books by Clare Connelly

Harlequin Presents

Emergency Marriage to the Greek
Pregnant Princess in Manhattan
The Boss's Forbidden Assistant
Twelve Nights in the Prince's Bed

Passionately Ever After...

Cinderella in the Billionaire's Castle

The Long-Lost Cortéz Brothers

The Secret She Must Tell the Spaniard
Desert King's Forbidden Temptation

Brooding Billionaire Brothers

The Sicilian's Deal for "I Do"
Contracted and Claimed by the Boss

The Diamond Club

His Runaway Royal

Visit the Author Profile page
at Harlequin.com for more titles.

PREGNANT BEFORE THE PROPOSAL

CLARE CONNELLY

Harlequin

PRESENTS

Harlequin®
PRESENTS™

ISBN-13: 978-1-335-93918-0

Pregnant Before the Proposal

Copyright © 2024 by Clare Connelly

Recycling programs for this product may not exist in your area.

For questions and comments about the quality of this book, please contact us at CustomerService@Harlequin.com.

TM and ® are trademarks of Harlequin Enterprises ULC.

 Harlequin Enterprises ULC
22 Adelaide St. West, 41st Floor
Toronto, Ontario M5H 4E3, Canada
www.Harlequin.com

Printed in Lithuania

MIX
Paper | Supporting responsible forestry
www.fsc.org FSC® C021394

PREGNANT BEFORE THE PROPOSAL

To Megan Haslam

Who commissioned my first Harlequin and has been the most incredible partner ever since. We've worked together on more than forty books and I have adored the process each and every time, and learned so, so much from your generously shared wisdom. Thank you for always seeing the essence of the stories I wanted to tell, and helping me to carve that out better, tighter, more emotionally. You are a superstar!

CHAPTER ONE

LIBBY CURSED UNDER her breath at the unmistakable and unexpected sensation of the luxury yacht *moving*. Not moving in the gentle, bob-bob-bob way it was supposed to whilst moored at the marina, but rather like a bull at a gate, out of the dock, at high speed.

She stood, then almost fell, as the boat veered hard left.

Removing one of her yellow gloves, Libby placed it, along with the microfibre cloth she'd been using to dust beneath the Spanish Revival desk in the centre of the luxuriously appointed office, down on the floor and planted her feet a little wider.

They were *not* supposed to be moving.

At least, not while she was on board.

Her eyes flew to the clock across the room.

Her cleaning shift had another hour to go and Libby was supposed to be completely alone. Only she wasn't. When she'd come onboard, it had been to discover that the owner of the craft, whom she'd been told would be at an event in the city, was actually *in situ*, all swarthy, brooding billionaire.

It hadn't bothered Libby *per se*, though she generally

preferred solitude—the habit of a lifetime was hard to shake.

Now, she realised there was someone else. Or many someone elses.

Outside the corridor of the office, she could hear raised voices. Shouting. Her ears pricked up, listening to the foreign language. Spanish? Italian?

She whirled around, looking for somewhere to hide, something to grab to defend herself with if necessary. She grabbed a paperweight then ran behind the desk, to hide beneath it. Many were the times in Libby Langham's twenty-six years when she'd wished for a few extra inches, but this was not one of them. The space wasn't huge and yet it easily accommodated her petite frame.

With great effort she stilled her breath, and though she was no longer a five-year-old with a penchant for playing hide and seek, she clenched her eyes shut, willing away whatever dangers might come her way.

The door burst open. More shouting—the voices of several men. Then the sound of skin connecting with skin and the slamming of the door.

She kept her eyes squeezed shut, the paperweight in her hand heavy and smooth, somehow comforting, and she waited, listening.

Footsteps.

Heavy breathing.

A curse rang through the air, gruff and hoarse, the language foreign, and yet she could easily discern it was a swearword from the harsh inflection.

Fear rose in her chest like a tidal wave, threatening to devour her.

She heard pacing, another expulsion of breath, and

then a rasped, accented voice commanded, 'You can come out of there now.'

Her crystal blue eyes opened in alarm but naturally she stayed where she was, the fingers of one hand crossing in the hope of good luck.

'You're the cleaner, *si*?'

Her heart sank, but at the same time something like relief flooded her. This was the owner of the boat; she was almost sure of it. She didn't know his name—the company had simply given her the address and hourly rate—but he'd nodded a greeting when she'd come on-board, said a curt 'hello', before returning to his work. His voice sounded close enough to the same.

She'd wondered at the time if it was some kind of Hollywood heavyweight—not unheard of in this uber luxe Sydney marina. He certainly had the looks of a film star. Though he was rough around the edges, she mused, not at all styled and primped. There was a rawness to him that was almost primal, that—

'Do you speak English?'

Her train of thought was interrupted by his abrupt query.

With shaking legs, Libby pushed up from under the desk, wiping her un-gloved hand down the front of her uniform as she scanned the room quickly.

Yes. It was the same man she'd seen when she came aboard a couple of hours earlier. He was formally dressed for being on a yacht—in suit trousers and a white button-down shirt that was pushed up to the elbows. His shoes were gleaming.

'We have a situation,' he said darkly, crossing his arms over his chest.

'So I gathered.' She was pleased to have finally been able to locate her voice. Her tongue darted out, licking her lower lip. 'What's happening?'

'Four men have taken over the—' he paused as the yacht lurched quickly and the man's eyes swept shut '—boat,' he finished. 'Though God only knows what will be left of it when they are finished.' His nostrils flared with indignation.

'You're hurt,' she said, just realising that his cheek was bruised.

The man lifted his fingers, absent-mindedly tracing the line of his cheekbone. 'It's not important.'

She bit down on her lip. 'Do you need something?'

His brow furrowed and his eyes—a deep, dark grey— regarded her with a hint of mockery. 'Do you happen to have an ice pack in your pockets?'

'Well, no,' she finished lamely, cheeks heating at having been caught out. 'I just—'

'I'm fine,' he interrupted, reaching down and scooping up her glove and cloth. 'And next time you want to hide, you should take all the evidence with you.' He handed them to her.

Libby winced, feeling stupid, which she hated more than anything. How many stepfathers had made her feel like a fool? Some had simply ignored her; others had tolerated her with obvious impatience. Those men had been bad enough. But there were the ones who'd been genuinely unkind, who'd seemed to delight in berating Libby, in pointing out her every mistake, just because she was thoughtful and considered and liked to know what she was talking about before she spoke.

Spinning around to hide her expression, she walked a little away from him. 'Have you tried calling for help?'

'They took my phone, naturally. But you—'

'Yes, I have one,' she said, fumbling in her pocket and removing it. 'No signal.'

'It doesn't matter. The emergency number will work, it routes through satellite. Give it to me.'

It didn't even occur to her to argue. The man had such a natural authority, it was easy to believe that he could somehow make everything better.

She watched as he called, her eyes flitting every now and again to the locked door, ears straining for any noise that might indicate the pirates were returning.

He spoke with easy command, describing the boat to the last detail, plus his best guess of their current position and likely destination. He also described the four assailants, from their approximate ages to heights, plus his own location on the boat.

'I am here with someone—a cleaner.' Covering the mouthpiece, 'What is your name?'

'Libby.' She cleared her throat. 'Libby Langham.'

'And is there any family you need contacted?'

She blanched, shaking her head. No family. Not for Libby. She had been alone a long time; she was used to it. And if her mother's string of failed relationships had taught her anything, it was that being alone was preferable to the never-ending cycle of fast love and traumatic breakups. She might have been lonely, but at least she wasn't hurting.

His eyes skimmed her face for a moment, sending her stomach dropping to the floor, and then he finished the call. 'I will attempt to contain the situation before you arrive—'

Evidently, whoever was on the other end of the call didn't think that was such a great idea, but the man—Raul, he'd said his name at the start of the conversation, Libby remembered—was not to be dissuaded.

'Then you had better send help swiftly.'

He disconnected the call but held the phone in the palm of his hand, contemplating.

'What did they say?' she asked, fidgeting anxiously.

'They're sending police.' He paced the room. 'This is not the first boat theft in the area—which is something the marina should have mentioned, don't you think?'

Libby grimaced. 'It would have been nice.'

'You work here. Have you experienced this?'

She laughed, though it wasn't funny. 'Being hijacked at high speed? No. But we've literally just taken over the contract for the marina. This is only my second job on a boat,' she said, aware that she was babbling.

His intelligent eyes scanned the surroundings, assessing. 'I'm going to go out there,' he said, moving across the room, twisting the doorknob and confirming that it was locked.

'No way. That's madness.'

He arched a brow.

'You have no idea if they're armed, nor what they're capable of. The police are on their way. Just…wait it out.'

His nostrils flared. 'I was caught unawares before, but I will not be again. You stay here.'

She swallowed past a lump in her throat. 'I'm not going to let you go and take on all the risk.'

'It's my boat,' he pointed out. 'You're just caught in the crosshairs.'

'Yes, but I *am* caught in the crosshairs, so don't do anything stupid.'

'They are just kids,' he snapped. 'Idiotic, stupid children. I know, because I was one once. Don't worry. I can handle myself.'

She shook her head, wondering why she *was* so worried. After all, it was his life, his choice to do whatever he wanted with it.

'Fine, but I'm going with you,' she said boldly, earning a sharp laugh of derision.

'Very brave, Libby Langham, but I suspect you'd quickly become a liability.'

'I'm tougher than I look,' she responded, smarting from his retort. Little did he know, she'd had to toughen up from a young age.

His nostrils flared. 'Stay here.'

'No way. If you go, I'm going.'

He glared at her.

'How are you going to get out, anyway?' she pushed. 'The door's locked.'

He threw her a look. 'I'm sure I can deal with that.'

'So you're going to what? Kick it down?'

He arched a brow. 'Don't think I can?'

She shook her head. 'What if they're on the other side?'

'Then you'd better grab your paperweight again,' he said, half mocking. 'How good is your aim?'

She was tempted to ask him to stay still and she'd let him know, but her nerves were stretched to breaking point.

'I'm serious,' she said quietly. 'What's your plan? Just to go all Rambo on them?'

'Why not?'

She eyed him consideringly. He definitely had the physique of someone who could handle themselves and for all she knew, he had the skills too.

'What are your chances?'

He surprised her then by pacing across the room and stopping right in front of her. 'Let's just say I never back away from a challenge.'

'What does that mean?' she murmured. Up close, she was aware of the way his eyes were more than just grey, they were almost silver or gold, with specks of luminescence made all the more noticeable by his thick, dark lashes, which seemed to form perfect frames.

'My chances are good, Libby. But they're better if you stay here.'

'Don't count on it,' she muttered and, though she was afraid, she knew there was no way she was going to remain hidden in the office while he went and put his life on the line.

The boat jerked hard to the left, knocking them both a little off-balance. Libby might have fallen altogether if Raul hadn't pressed out his hand and caught her elbow, steadying her, holding her just long enough to make sure she was safe. But it was more than long enough.

Heat radiated through her skin, over her body, adrenalin firing in her veins.

'Let's do this,' she said with a nod, gaze darting towards the door.

His eyes narrowed, inspecting hers. 'On one condition.'

She waited.

'Do exactly as I say. And stay behind me.'

'That's two.'

He shook his head. 'Don't make me regret this.'

'You *should* regret this,' she said. 'You have no idea—'

'We could both be dead before the police get here, the way they're steering this thing,' he pointed out. 'You think being down here and waiting for help makes us any safer?'

She bit into her lower lip, shaking her head. 'I guess not.'

'Good. So?'

'Fine,' she agreed, though she crossed her fingers behind her back. She'd do whatever she needed to in the moment, and if Raul didn't like it he'd just have to lump it.

It was obvious that he still had some misgivings but, to his credit, he silenced them, moving to the door, giving it a shake once more, then leaning closer, listening for any noises beyond. He crouched down, eyes lined up with the small gap between the carpet and the timber. It was strange to notice something so superficial in a moment such as that, but Libby couldn't help the way her eyes dropped to his bottom and lingered there, her mouth suddenly dry as she appreciated the strength of his haunches, and his overtly masculine form.

'See anything?' she asked, close to his feet, voice surprisingly thin.

'Nothing,' he confirmed.

'Okay, good.' She quickly looked away, blinking to clear her mind of the imagery of his rear end. 'That's good, right?'

He stood, tilting a look at her. 'Yes, it's good. Stand back.'

She did as he said, taking a few paces away from the door, relieved to put some space between them.

Raul turned to her. 'I don't know where they are—obviously, at least one of them is on the deck, perhaps all. Perhaps they'll hear the door opening. Be prepared for anything, got it?'

She nodded, nerves making it impossible to speak.

'Got your paperweight?'

She pulled a face. 'Are you making fun of me?'

'On the contrary, it's an excellent weapon. Keep it, in case you need to defend yourself.'

Her eyes widened. 'Do you think—'

'I don't know,' he said sharply. 'If you would prefer to stay here and let me handle this, I would welcome that choice.'

'No,' she demurred, reaching for the paperweight, then returning to the middle of the room.

He frowned, turned his attention back to the door, and ran at it, kicking his leg at the last moment, with the skill and precision of a man who might have done so every day of his life.

The door splintered a little at the frame, but it gave quickly and easily. Raul moved fast, his hand catching the door even as he dropped his foot to the floor, to prevent it from slamming loudly against the wall.

Then, needlessly, he turned back to Libby, lifting a finger to his lips to remind her to be quiet.

With a pulse that was racing so hard she could hardly think straight, she fell into step behind him. At the end of the corridor, he lifted his finger to his lips again, before pulling open a door beneath the steps.

She looked around anxiously as he disappeared inside.

A moment later, he returned with some orange rope and nets.

'Let me guess,' she hissed. 'You were a Boy Scout in another life.'

His smirk did something funny to her stomach. 'Not quite. Ready?'

She nodded, though how could she be? She had no idea what was coming next.

'Wait for my signal,' he murmured, climbing the steps stealthily. At the top, he slowed, looked around, climbed higher, until he'd disappeared altogether, then his hand appeared, gesturing for her to follow.

She did, swallowed, stumbling on one step and wincing at the noise, waiting to make sure nothing happened because of it. But the engine was too loud, and the waves were crashing against the side of the boat; there was no way they'd be heard.

They emerged onto the back of the deck.

'They're together,' he said. 'We have the element of surprise. Plus,' he said, glancing through the windows before crouching down, 'they look drunk.'

She nodded. 'You're sure you don't want to just wait?'

The boat turned hard right, and Libby opened her mouth to squeal because it tipped at such an angle she genuinely thought they might capsize. It was only Raul's hand—broad and capable, warm and strong—over her mouth that silenced her.

She stared into his eyes—eyes that were loaded with warning and confidence, that told her to be quiet, all would be well—and she found herself, weirdly, believing in him.

'We can't wait,' he said. 'Believe me when I tell you:

we'll be doing them a favour too. They evidently have a death wish.'

She lifted her head the smallest amount so she could see inside the windows, and realised that Raul had been right. They were little more than teenagers. Raul and Libby had a moral imperative to save them from themselves.

She eyed the paperweight sceptically; she'd be unlikely to use it.

'Keep it,' he said, as if reading her thoughts. 'Just in case.'

And then he smiled. A smile that was dazzling and beautiful and which somehow managed to assuage all her doubts and anxieties. 'Follow me.'

In that moment she was pretty sure she'd follow him into the very fires of hell if he asked it of her...

CHAPTER TWO

HE WAS LIKE a hurricane, a phenomenon of strength and precision that came almost entirely out of nowhere, bursting into the control room of his mega yacht as though he'd been born fighting. There were four men and only one Raul, but Raul went for the biggest teenager, clearly the ringleader, shoving him away from the controls and standing with his legs braced, eyeing up the group, who looked shocked and, yes, drunk.

'Right—' he spoke with stern command '—get over there.'

The oldest, rubbing his shoulder, where it had connected with the wall, glared back. 'Who's gonna make us?'

'Believe me, you don't want the answer to that question.' His accent grew thicker. 'I am giving you a chance to end this peacefully,' he said, reaching behind them and bringing the boat to a halt. Libby saw him remove the key and slip it in his pocket.

Clever.

The feeling of stillness after such a chaotic and wild ride was a huge relief. She held her ground, wary and watchful but oddly not feeling in any danger.

Raul just seemed so completely in control, it was mesmerising.

'Yeah, well, you're outnumbered,' one of the smaller teens said, bravely approaching Raul. 'Come on, we can take him.'

'I wouldn't bet on it,' Raul replied, and when the teen lifted his fist and attempted to land another punch, Raul caught it, twisting it quickly and sharply up the boy's back.

'Stay back,' he warned another of the group, who'd made to move closer. Then, turning to Libby, 'Come here, please.'

It took her a moment to galvanise her feet into action, but after a small pause, she skirted around the edge of the group towards Raul.

'Take the rope. Tie this one up.'

She nodded, moving as quickly as she could with fingers that were shaking, while Raul continued to restrain the teen's hands and stare down the rest of the thieves, who were clearly running out of fight.

'We didn't know you'd be on board,' the fourth one to speak muttered. 'It was meant to be empty.'

'My plans changed,' Raul snapped. 'But, either way, this was not an open invitation for you to take my boat and almost destroy it.'

'We didn't—'

He glared at the ringleader. 'Enough. Go and sit down against the wall, hands behind your back.'

Libby's pulse was racing in her ears. Was it really possible this could be over so easily?

Apparently not. At the exact moment she began to relax, one of the smaller teens lunged towards her, grabbing her around the neck, and she startled and might have screamed, except she had Raul's warning in her mind that she would be a liability and she didn't want to prove him right.

And so she thought quickly, stomped her foot down onto the boy's toes as hard as she could, then lifted her knee and connected it with a sensitive part of his anatomy. He dropped to the ground, curled into a ball.

'Effective technique,' Raul drawled with approval. 'Anyone else want a lesson from Libby?'

'We didn't know you'd be on board,' the ringleader said again.

'And how exactly did you become privy to his schedule?' Libby demanded, emboldened by her success in subduing the would-be attacker.

'I—'

'Shut up, Jerry,' the smallest of the group shouted.

Raul's eyes locked onto Libby's with something like admiration.

'Let me guess. One of you has a friend who works at the marina.' Her eyes widened. 'Or for the cleaning contractor!' she said, snapping her fingers. 'Of course. How else would you know anything about the boat owner's commitments?'

Raul moved then to subdue the third boy, tying his hands easily before moving to the fourth. 'Sit down,' he commanded. 'And don't say anything.'

Turning back to Libby, he murmured, 'Watch them.' Then, more quietly, 'Are you okay?'

She nodded, and she was, though she could feel the start of her adrenalin turning into something else, her throat thickening with emotion at what had just happened.

Raul inserted the key into the boat and thrummed the engine to life. A moment later, they were cruising back towards the marina—at high speed, but with absolute safety and command. Libby tried not to take her eyes off the delinquents, but every now and again she sneaked a glance at Raul and felt her pulse wobble.

He'd gone into survival mode. The same strengths and instincts that had kept him alive on the streets of Spain as a runaway street kid had thundered to life once more, fine-tuning his responses so that he acted purely with one objective in mind: survival. Not just his own survival, but Libby's too.

The yacht under his control once more, the gang subdued and contrite-looking, Raul allowed himself to glance once in Libby's direction, noticing things he'd been too under pressure to conceive of at the time.

From her shimmering blonde hair to icy blue eyes, petite frame and honey-gold skin, full and pouting lips, and natural athleticism—which he'd witnessed for himself as she'd prepared to go toe to toe with the teen who'd attacked her.

Her eyes lifted to his and caught him staring. He smiled slowly, a quirk of his mouth. Her lips parted, showing a full, perfect circle, and he felt something tighten in his groin.

Adrenalin of a wholly different nature fired to life. He recognised it well.

The thrill of victory, of survival, made him feel more alive than almost anything else.

It was a thrill he remembered. Now his victories tended to be in the boardroom rather than on the streets.

At first, that had been thrilling, but in recent years he'd become complacent even with his biggest corporate wins.

'We just thought—'

Raul turned his attention back to one of the teens, a stab of sympathy shifting through him.

'You didn't think,' he said quietly. 'You tried to take what you wanted, and you could have all got yourselves killed in the process.'

The teen dropped his head.

The marina was in view now, complete with flashing lights, indicating the water police were in action. He pulled the yacht towards a pontoon, concentrating on the manoeuvre as well as on the teens.

As soon as the boat came to a stop there was the sound of thudding boots on the deck and then police were bursting into the control room, sweeping it with loud noises, guns held.

'I am the owner,' Raul announced, palms lifted. 'This is my boat.'

Libby, he saw, echoed his gesture, lifting her hands.

'These are the four you're after.'

'Do you have some identification, sir?' the more senior of the officers queried.

Raul reached into his pocket and removed a slimline wallet, from which he brandished a driving licence. The officer took it, looking from Raul to the photograph then nodding.

'And you?' He turned to Libby.

'She's with me,' Raul said, surprised at the possessive heat that stole through him. Then again, Libby had stood shoulder to shoulder with him in the midst of whatever danger might have befallen him. Naturally he felt a connection with her.

'Righto. Take 'em out,' the officer said with a nod. 'I'll need you to make a statement. Do you require medical attention?'

'He was punched,' Libby said, and Raul almost laughed at her concern.

'I'm reasonably sure I'll survive though,' he drawled, moving closer to her unconsciously. 'Are you okay?'

She nodded once.

'So you're happy to make a statement now?'

Raul looked down at Libby. She was shaking. Predictably, shock was setting in.

'A brief statement,' he said with a nod. 'And by brief, I mean five minutes. I can provide more tomorrow.'

The officer opened his mouth as if to argue but then he nodded. 'Of course.' He pulled out his notepad and asked for the bare outline of events. Raul detailed what had happened. Libby nodded. It was over quickly. The officer handed Raul his card. 'If you remember anything else, give me a call.'

Raul's eyes glittered. 'Count on it.'

As quickly as it had begun, it was over. The officers left, the sirens stopped, and they were alone. Libby's adrenalin had completely evaporated now and she found herself shaking from head to toe.

'I…should go,' she said, turning to Raul, frowning, because it had truly been the strangest afternoon of her life.

'No, I forbid it,' Raul responded, his lips twisting in a half-smile, yet his voice was deathly serious. 'Sit.' He

guided her into the captain's chair then disappeared, returning a moment later with a blanket, which he wrapped
around her shoulders, before leaving once more.

When he came back it was with a tumbler of Scotch.
'Drink this.'

Libby wrinkled her nose. 'I'm not really one for hard
liquor.'

'Desperate times,' he said, with a quiet gentleness to
his voice.

Her gaze was drawn to his and something exploded in
her chest. It was the strangest feeling! As though something in the very depths of her soul recognised something within him, calling to her, making her trust him
implicitly.

She reached out, taking the Scotch, eyes latching
onto his and holding as she lifted the tumbler to her lips
and tasted it. Shuddering a little, she let the liquid touch
her tongue, discovering there was something pleasing
about it after all, something steadying to her nerves. She
scrunched up her face and drank the rest, then coughed
as it hit her palate like a Molotov cocktail.

'Okay?' He patted her back as he asked, crouching
down beside her, and this time, when their eyes met, everything inside her seemed to jolt into place. She was
floating and flying all at once. Her bones seemed to
turn to jelly.

She nodded, but she was shaking. From the terror of
what had just happened? Or from something else?

Strangely, she hadn't been afraid. Not once they'd entered the room and she'd seen how in control Raul was.
He'd made it all seem fine. Somehow, she'd just known
he would triumph. He had a quality; there was something

inherently trustworthy about him, something Libby had never really experienced first-hand in a man. Not her father, whom she'd never known, not any of the men her mother had dated, and not her first—and only—boyfriend.

She stared at Raul because it was impossible to look away.

'I feel—' she said, pressing a hand to the middle of her chest, frowning as she searched for the right word.

His eyes were shuttered, impossible to read. But something was bubbling up inside Libby. An awakening, something that was vitally important. It caught her completely off-guard because it ran contrary to all of her usual instincts. Having seen the way her mother flung herself headlong into romantic entanglements, Libby had very, very carefully always been the exact opposite. Oh, she wanted love, she craved it in many ways, but not like her mother had. When Libby fell in love it would be for keeps, with the right kind of man. Someone kind and gentle who wouldn't hurt her. She'd certainly never give in to something as superficial and unreliable as physical chemistry!

Yet now she felt desire running through her like a current, sucking her along with it, hypnotising her and seducing her, making her want to act on these impulses despite her better judgement. Was this what it had been like for her mother?

'Raul,' she said desperately, moving her hand from her own chest to his. 'You were incredible.' She heard the awe in her voice, the admiration, wondered if she should contain it, act cool or something. But she couldn't. 'I feel more alive than I've ever felt,' she said, smiling, and when his gaze dropped to her mouth she was propelled forward. There was an inevitability to it, a sense of rightness, and before she could overthink it and listen to the warning instincts that had kept her safe from heartbreak all these years, she brushed her lips to his, seeking connection.

She'd half-expected him to pull back. She felt him stiffen and knew he hadn't been anticipating her action. She hovered there, lips pressed to his, but not deepening the kiss, just breathing him in, wondering if she'd just made a colossal, embarrassing mistake.

But then, as if the same inevitability was driving Raul, suddenly he was kissing her too, with a visceral growl ripped from his chest, a hand coming to cup behind her head, holding her there for his pleasure, his tongue rolling hers, his lips commanding, demanding, perfection. They moved as one, her standing, or being pulled to standing, by Raul, his hands drawing her closer, into his chest, which was broad and rugged, and through which she could feel his heart beating rapidly.

It was like the bursting of a dam.

The tension and the danger of the preceding thirty minutes had accumulated to form a ground swell of need that was threatening to devour Libby, but in Raul there was salvation, there was relief.

His hands moved deftly, removing her clothing, and she didn't question how out of character this was, how strange; she simply went with the flow, surrendering to a moment that was so much bigger than her.

His chest was bare beneath her hands; she realised she'd done that, shucking his shirt then moving to his trousers, which he stepped out of at the same time she pushed at them. There was desperation in their movements and now they knelt in unison, then his body was over hers, hungry, urgent, his mouth demanding, his hands roaming her skin, touching every inch of her, worshipping her breasts until she could hardly breathe, his mouth following his fingers, chasing his kisses. She felt as though everything was spinning too fast, like she couldn't focus on anything beyond this.

But then he was moving, his body gone, and confusion swamped her. She pushed up on her elbows, watching as he unfolded his wallet, removed a condom and pressed it over his length.

Her eyes widened, because he was huge and she hadn't done this in a long time, and even then only a few times, and hadn't really enjoyed it, so in the midst of the inevitability of this, something sharp jabbed her consciousness, making her doubt.

She should stop this.

She wasn't her mother.

She'd learned her lessons all too well.

Except she hadn't, apparently, because she was burning up with need and desire and her brain refused to listen. Raul came back to her, and so did her certainty, her need, pushing everything else away, so when he separated her legs with his knee she felt only excitement. Then he was pushing into her and she was crying out with a surge of something she'd never known before, as all the life-affirming feelings of relief, adrenalin, need and power thrilled in her veins. He kissed her as he moved and she wrapped her legs around his waist, the sublime perfection of this moment somehow totally appropriate after the strange detour her day had already taken. Later, she'd probably wonder what had come over her, but for now, all Libby could do was lie there and enjoy the best pleasure she'd ever known…

'Well,' he drawled, moving away from her with true regret but knowing he needed to put some distance between them if he were to have any hope of regaining his sanity. 'That was unexpected.'

To his relief, Libby smiled. A slow, sensual smile. 'Which part? The boat being stolen, or the sex?'

Amusement flickered in the pit of his belly. 'Both.'

'Agreed.' She looked around the control room, her lips turning down as the wild tangle of their clothes became evident.

'I think in the heat of the moment—'

'The relief of having survived,' she agreed, nodding.

He was glad she was being so sensible, that she saw things as he did, so why was there also a hint of frustration that she was so quick to dismiss this?

Raul was flying out of the country the next day, it wasn't as though he could offer her anything more, not like he would want to, anyway.

'It was all…surreal,' she said with a lift of her brows.

'But wonderful,' he murmured, pulling on his shorts and crouching down. 'The second part, anyway.'

Heat flushed her cheeks, a sweet innocence that made him wonder how often she did this sort of thing. She hadn't been a virgin, but there was something about her totally unguarded responses that made him wonder…

He shut down the thoughts.

He didn't wonder about the women he slept with. He

didn't postulate on their private lives. He had sex, and he moved on.

'Are you okay?'

She nodded, expelling a soft sigh.

'I mean after the whole boat hijacking incident. No injuries?'

She shook her head.

'Sometimes, these things can build as a trauma inside of you. If you should find you experience this, and need help, I want you to let me know.'

Her eyes widened. 'I'm sure I'll be fine,' she mumbled.

'I am too. Nonetheless...' He moved to his wallet, ignoring the other condom in there with great willpower. 'Here's my card.'

She took it without looking down. 'Thanks.'

He nodded once, feeling that at least he'd done his duty there. 'Suffice it to say, I'll cover any expenses. Therapy, whatever you need.'

She laughed then. 'Raul, it's fine. I'm fine.' She stood, retrieving her underwear, dressing with a litheness of movement that made his mouth dry. She was so effortlessly graceful, she was beautiful to watch.

He frowned. 'Would you care to have dinner with me?'

Her eyes widened as though it was the last thing she'd been expecting him to say. And wasn't that true for him too? Dinner? After sex?

He could only put the uncharacteristic offer down to the bizarre day he'd had.

'It's too early for dinner,' she pointed out, waving a hand towards the sky. She was right. It probably wasn't even six yet. 'And I'm not hungry.' She finished dress-ing. 'I'll just get my things and go.'

After the storm came the calm, and in that calm she had space to freak out, just a little, at what had happened. While sleeping with Raul had been incredible, it had also been totally unlike Libby, and she found herself jangling with nerves and needing some space to be alone.

The idea of sharing dinner with him made something ache in the pit of her stomach. She couldn't say why, only that she felt his gravitational pull and saw danger in it, a danger that surprised her with its intensity, because a moment ago she'd been thinking that he was safety and trust personified.

Frustrated with her ambivalence and lack of clarity, she pushed a bright smile to her face, hoping it radiated with a confidence she was far from feeling.

'Well, it was…nice…if somewhat strange, to meet you,' she said, and she held out her hand. It might have seemed like an odd thing to do, having just slept with him on the floor of his boat, but Libby needed to reas-sert herself as a confident, sensible woman—the exact opposite of her mother in every way.

'You too, Libby Langham.' He took her hand and a shiver ran all the way from her fingertips to her heart, making her tremble. She quickly pulled her hand away and spun before he could see it. She needed to get out of there.

'You can't be serious?' The police detective regarded Raul as though he'd sprouted three heads.

'Why not?' Raul didn't move, not even a little. He held his expression, his stance and, most of all, his mettle.

'Well, it's just…unusual, that's all. I mean, they tried to steal a multi-million-dollar boat from you,' the detective pointed out, drawing a hand through his hair before gesturing towards Raul's face. 'Clocked you on the cheek. And you're offering to pay their school fees?'

'I'm offering whatever assistance they need,' he confirmed with a nod. 'I would like you to arrange a meeting with their parents for this afternoon.' He flicked a glance at his watch. He'd be flying out later tonight, so there was limited time in which to wrap this up. But having grown up poor and on the streets, Raul had also done things in his youth of which he was ashamed. He knew how easy it was to take a wrong turn in life, to make a mistake, particularly when no one believed you were capable of more. It was because of one couple's act of faith in him that Raul's life had forked in a better direction, and it was for them that he now tried to offer hope when he could to other children in similar situations to what his own had once been.

'These boys have been in and out of trouble most of their lives,' the detective repeated incredulously.

'All the more reason to try something new. Arrange the meeting—if they want help, I'm going to give it.'

He left the police station, satisfied with the steps he was planning to take for the youths, knowing it was the right thing to do. And yet there was a sense of impatience in his belly too, a feeling of wanting more.

Of wanting Libby.

His mind flashed back to the boat, to their time together, and he closed his eyes for a moment as a wave

of desire washed over him, remembered pleasure holding him completely in its thrall, and then he was moving, determinedly pushing the whole experience from
his mind and focusing on his next destination, his next
conquest, his next challenge. Raul didn't look back, he
didn't do repeat experiences and, most importantly, he
didn't stick around anywhere—or anyone—long enough
to get attached.

CHAPTER THREE

Three months later

IT WAS A miracle she'd even kept the business card, because Lord knew she'd had no intention of calling Raul for help. Perhaps it had been a sort of talisman, proof that she hadn't imagined the whole thing. Yet she hadn't looked at it again. She'd placed the card into her wallet and then ignored it.

Every time she'd gone to pay for something, her fingers might have glanced over the edges of the thing, but she'd never once weakened and removed it, looked at it and invoked an image of Raul Ortega. Then again, she hardly needed a business card for that.

He was burned into her brain in a way she found quite frustrating, given the brevity of their acquaintance. She only had to close her eyes to see his, to remember the way he'd felt, smelled, tasted...

And now, she thought, with a whole heap of butterflies terrorising her belly, what was she to do?

She glanced down at her lap, to the white stick with two bright pink lines, and felt a desperate sense of panicked disbelief rising inside of her.

Pregnant!

How could it be?

They'd used protection!

It had only happened once!

They barely even knew each other!

It was... She shook her head. Inevitable?

Even as she thought it, she knew it was stupid, and wrong. Nothing about this should have been inevitable. It shouldn't have happened.

She groaned, pressing her head back against the threadbare sofa cushions, tears filling her eyes even as a protective hand shifted to cover her still-flat stomach.

It was history repeating herself, she thought with a groan. Libby had been an accident too. She'd been raised by a single mother, had never known nor met her father. She'd never even been sure her mother knew who he was. If she had, the older woman had scrupulously avoided revealing that to Libby.

She patted her stomach, the connection she felt to the burgeoning life unmistakable and immediate. It was something she'd never really felt before.

She'd loved her mother, almost out of a sense of obligation. Children loved their parents—that's just how it was. Only they'd never been close, and now that Libby looked back she recognised that she'd been the responsible person of the household for almost as long as she could remember. Grocery shopping and meal preparations had mostly fallen to her, so too the cleaning. Between school and those domestic duties, Libby had been too tired for a normal teenage experience, and as for thoughts of university...? No way. It wouldn't have been possible.

And now, just when she felt like her life was stabilis-

ing, she was looking down the barrel of single parenthood, with no possible support network, no safety net.

Just like her mother had been, she realised with a
groan. After all her best endeavours to be *different*, to
make different choices, to live a different life, here she
was facing the exact same predicament.

It horrified her.

Libby wrapped her arms around her chest, shivering despite the warmth of the day, then flicked another
glance at Raul's business card.

She was terrified to tell him, terrified not to tell him:
she was simply terrified in every way.

New York glittered like a million stars, bright and beautiful, but Raul barely saw it. He'd sworn he'd never take
things like this for granted. Not when he was working
his ass off to get ahead, not when he was on his way up.
But success and wealth were impossible not to become
accustomed to, and after almost a decade as a billionaire,
nowadays, Raul didn't tend to see the opulence and rare
privilege afforded to him.

The stunning vista was simply a backdrop to the work
he was doing, and he had more interest in his computer
screen than the Empire State Building.

When his phone began to ring, he was tempted to ignore it, except it was his most private line, the number
he gave out only rarely.

If someone was calling him on this number, it was
important.

He reached for the receiver, cradling it beneath his
chin. 'Ortega,' he grunted into the phone, eyes still lingering on the screen.

Outside, it had begun to snow, little drifts of white dancing in front of the window, but he didn't notice. If he'd moved to the glass and looked all the way down, if he'd been able to see so far beneath him, it would have been to appreciate the looks of wonder on children's faces, delight all 'round.

'Hello?' he prompted, impatient now. He had until midnight to file these documents; he didn't intend to miss the window.

'Erm, hi.' The voice was soft and familiar, even though he couldn't immediately place it. Yet his body reacted, his gut tightening, something popping in the depths of his belly.

'Who is this?' he asked, guarded. Anyone who could make him react so instinctively deserved his wariness.

Silence.

Heavy breathing.

He gripped the phone more tightly, but then there was simply a dial tone.

Whoever it was had hung up.

Now he did stand, jack-knifing out of his chair and striding towards the window, standing with legs wide and hands in his pockets, staring out, not seeing. A sense of unease slipped through him, as though he'd just missed something, or someone, important.

Libby knew she was being a coward, but hearing his voice again had flooded her with such a ball of tension she could hardly think straight, much less speak.

On the day they'd met, she'd been blown away by his sense of command and authority. But those same things had flown down the phone line when she'd called him, and they'd knocked her sideways.

She couldn't help but feel that she was about to throw a bomb into his life, and all that natural authority would be turned on her. She needed to form a more definitive plan first, so that when she did tell him about the baby, and he asked what she wanted to do, she could respond with a degree of certainty.

It was in the small hours of the morning that the answer came to him.

Strangely, it wasn't so much her voice as the husky little breaths she'd exhaled into the phone line. They'd been familiar in a primal way, triggering a sense memory that had lain dormant for months. But once back in the privacy of his home, naked in his bed, he remembered, and a hot flash spread through his body as every cell reverberated with surprise. Surprise at the pleasure he'd felt at hearing her voice, at the knowledge that she'd called him after all.

And then concern. Because if she was calling him, surely it meant something was wrong.

When he reflected on the details of the day, contemplated how traumatic it must have been for Libby, he knew he needed to make sure she was okay. He should have done so before now, he realised with a sense of shame, only he'd never taken her phone number, he'd simply given her his.

And she'd used it.

No longer tired, despite the fact he'd been up since early the previous morning, he pushed back the sheet and began to make plans, setting things in motion so that he could as-sure himself Libby hadn't suffered as a result of that day…

So the morning sickness wasn't just for mornings, Libby thought with a shake of her head as she gingerly straight-ened and stared at her reflection in the bathroom mir-ror. Having battled nausea all day, finding her appetite almost non-existent, she'd forced herself to eat a piece of Vegemite toast when she got home from work, sim-ply because she figured she had to have something for the sake of the baby, but it hadn't settled her tummy as she'd hoped.

Quite the opposite.

The only silver lining was that she felt marginally bet-ter now, having showered and changed into a singlet top and floaty skirt. She was well enough, finally, to con-template a cup of tea. Moving to her kitchen, she flicked the kettle to life and stood, waiting for it to boil, eyes on the view beyond the kitchen window. At first glance, it was hardly inspiring. Just a brick wall to the neighbour-ing building. But it was the details that made Libby's heart lighten. The bougainvillea that clung to the sides, bursting with green leaves and bright pink flowers, the graffiti someone had done a few months back, a picture of a puppy dog in a hot-air balloon, and the way one of the residents had artfully strung their laundry from their window to a back fence, surely in contravention of some building code or other, but from where Libby stood, the sight of the summery linen clothes drying on the line was like a still-life painting.

The kettle flicked off and she splashed boiling water into the cup, watching as the colour seeped from the bag and into the tea, stifling a yawn. She was always tired at the moment, though doing double shifts at work every day for the last week hardly helped matters.

Nonetheless, Libby was abundantly conscious of the ticking time bomb of her pregnancy. She needed to start saving—and fast—if she was going to be able to take off a few months when the baby came.

And then what?

Her mind began to spin so fast she felt giddy.

She needed to find a job she could do from home, that much was clear. Cleaning for the agency was off the cards. She could take in ironing—another skill she possessed in abundance—but the idea was anathema to Libby. While she *could* iron, she hated it, and knew she'd turn to that only as a last resort.

So what else was there?

She flicked a glance over her shoulder at the fridge, where the pamphlet for the local adult education campus was printed. She'd circled the bookkeeping diploma months ago, even before she'd met Raul and shared that one fateful afternoon with him, but the idea of undertaking night school and picking up that skill was both terrifying and somehow imperative.

Could she do it? Libby bit down on her lip, pressing a hand to her belly.

The truth was, she didn't know. She'd never had the luxury of pushing herself academically. Her mother had wanted her to drop out of school in grade ten, so she could start 'contributing' to the household financially. Libby had held fast though. There weren't many things she'd been willing to go into bat for, but graduating high school was one of them. It had been exhausting and stressful, and she knew deep down that she could have got much better grades if she'd been allowed to study at night, but she'd had to content herself with passing.

But now? What was stopping her from enrolling in a course? True, it would be exhausting, but at least she'd have a sense of accomplishment, and the prospect of being able to support her child.

She pulled the milk from the fridge and added a splash to her tea, but midway through returning the bottle there was a sharp knock on her door. Her heart started at the un-expected interruption and she glanced out of the kitchen window, but whoever it was had moved into the alcove, shielding them from sight.

Desperate for her tea, she took a quick sip, exclaiming a little when it scalded her tongue, then moved through the small apartment to the door, wrenching it inwards with a polite smile on her face...

Which immediately dropped at the sight of Raul Ortega on the other side.

Her lips parted and everything went wonky in her mind. Libby's eyes seemed to fill with bright, radiant light.

'Raul,' she breathed out, gripping the door more tightly, needing it for strength and support. 'What are you doing here?' she whispered, blinking quickly. Was she imagining this?

'You called,' he responded, and Libby's heartrate ratcheted up.

'Oh...' she mumbled, her tummy twisting painfully.

'I presumed you needed something.'

Anxiety burst through her. He wasn't supposed to be here! This wasn't a conversation she wanted to have face to face. Or at all, if she could help it. Except she'd known, almost as soon as she'd discovered her pregnancy, that she wouldn't keep her child from his or her father, nor the father from her child. While Libby intended to be the primary caregiver, she would never stand in the way of the formation of such an important, foundational relationship.

So of course she *had* to tell him, and she had fully intended to, when the time was right. She just needed to build her courage up.

Except he was standing right in front of her, staring at her, lips pursed with a hint of impatience, and all the air whooshed right out of her lungs.

'Raul,' she said, as though it were a lifeline. As though by repeating his name everything might start to make sense.

But it didn't.

Had he come to Sydney just because she'd called? Or had he already been here? Surely the latter. There was no way he would have flown to Australia on the back of a ten-second call that essentially amounted to a prank.

Was it possible they'd been in the same city for weeks, months, and not known that a new life was forming of their inadvertent creation?

Sweat began to bead on the top of Libby's lip. She thought longingly of her tea.

'Why did you call?'

It was so imperious, so demanding. Just like she'd known him to be, only then his commanding nature had all been focused on the delinquent boys who'd stolen his yacht.

'I—' She darted her tongue out, licked her lower lip.

Libby had never felt more terrified in her life. Strange, when she'd been mentally gearing herself up for this conversation for over a week. As Raul's eyes dropped to her mouth and chased her tongue, though, something began to fizz in her belly then spread to her bloodstream, filling her with a tangle of emotions she couldn't fathom.

She sucked in a deep breath, tried to steady her nerves. 'You'd better come in,' she said, aiming for decisive and coming off loaded with dread. She cleared her throat. 'This…won't take long.'

His brow furrowed and he jammed his hands into his pockets, but he nodded once, curtly.

Curtly!

Her stomach dropped to her toes. She spun on her heel and moved inside her apartment, immediately ashamed of how shabby and small it was, aware of how it must look to his eyes. It had come partially furnished, so the sofa and small table weren't hers. She'd done her best to brighten up the place, covering the card table with colourful fabric and the sofa with a blanket she'd bought at an op shop, but it was, nonetheless, unmistakably cheap.

Not that she had any reason to apologise for her financial circumstances. If anything, Libby was proud of how she'd pulled herself up by the bootstraps. But Raul was…different…to anyone she'd ever known. Somehow, she didn't want him seeing her through this filter.

'I've just made a cup of tea. Would you like something to drink?' she asked nervously, pacing into the kitchen and wrapping her hands around the mug.

'No, thank you.' His frown deepened. 'How are you?'

'Fine,' she lied. 'Just fine. And you?'

He paused. 'Yes, also fine.'

But this was a disaster! Everything felt so strained and different to how it had been on the boat. Then adrenalin and adventure had been a great equaliser. She'd been emboldened by their shared experience, made brave and powerful by what they'd been through and how she'd shown her strength. Now her stomach was in knots and she had no idea how she could possibly get through the next few minutes. Only she knew she had to—somehow.

'Why did you call me, Libby?' he asked again, propping one hip against her kitchen counter.

The kitchen also showed signs of disrepair, but it was Libby's favourite room of the house, for the view it had of the beautiful bougainvillea and the way she'd brightly accessorised it so every surface popped with colour.

Drawing as much comfort from her surroundings as she possibly could, Libby sucked in a deep breath. 'I... thought you should know...' she began, then sipped her tea quickly. It had cooled down just enough to be palatable without burning.

'Yes?'

Her teeth pressed into her lip. 'God, this is way harder than it should be,' she said on a humourless laugh. If only he knew how much this was her worst nightmare. Not being pregnant, but all the circumstances surrounding it.

'Libby, are you okay?'

'No,' she groaned, placing her tea on the bench. 'Not really.' She frowned. 'And yes, at the same time.'

'That makes no sense.'

'I know,' she said softly, sucking in a deep breath. 'The thing is...' She stared at her tea rather than into his eyes, which were too perceptive, too inquisitive. Too *everything*. 'The thing is,' she started again. 'That day...'

Silence fell, except for the ticking of the clock, which sat on the kitchen bench. Strange, she'd never really noticed how imperious and loud it was before. Every second cranked noisily past.

'Raul, I'm pregnant,' she said finally, the words, now she'd committed to saying them, rushing out of her. 'Three and a half months pregnant, in fact. You're the father.'

CHAPTER FOUR

RAUL HAD OFTEN heard the expression 'the bottom fell out of someone's world', and he'd always thought it to be a slightly indulgent concept. He'd experienced many shocks in his life, many turns of event which had required him to dig deep and find his inner strength and determination, but he'd never once believed the bottom could fall out of his world.

Until that moment, when everything in his life lost its familiar shape and context, even his own self.

The universe shifted.

No! he wanted to shout. He wanted to reject her statement with every cell in his body. He wanted to pull apart the universe with his bare hands and shake this reality away. He *couldn't* be a father. Not to anyone. He couldn't be anything to anyone. He was a loner. Born that way, raised that way, he was better on his own.

His breathing grew rough and he stared at Libby, as if just by looking at her he could undo the words she'd spoken, or make better sense of them. As if by staring at her he could make sense of anything.

Her head was bent and the sun sliced through the kitchen, bathing her head in gold, like a halo. His eyes dropped of their own accord to her stomach. It was flat and neat, just as he remembered from that afternoon. She was naturally slim, but as he lifted his gaze back to her face his attention lingered on her breasts. Was he imagining them to be more rounded than they had been then? Was that proof of her assertion?

Was there any likelihood this wasn't true?

Why would she lie?

He'd used a condom, but that wasn't foolproof. He lifted a hand to his jaw, rubbing it across his chin, staring straight ahead without speaking. He'd been knocked sideways by her statement, but now his brain was clicking back into gear, spinning furiously fast in an attempt to analyse this properly.

She was clearly poor.

Her choice of occupation was hardly well paid, and her apartment was further proof that her means were stretched. Pregnancy might seem like a way to get some extra cash. Was that her end game?

Not that she'd planned this, of course. How could she have? The entire thing was spontaneous, brought on by the dramatic events of that day. He'd ensured, as he always did, that protection was used. He didn't ask if she was on contraception, he'd simply assumed a woman of her age would be, but that was obviously a stupid miscalculation.

'I see,' he said eventually, the words flattened of any emotion, even when he felt this news in the very core of his being.

Her head remained lowered, eyes shielded from him.

His brain whirled even as his body was in the midst of a classic fight or flight response.

Raul's instincts were shaped by his own experiences,

but he would not betray them until he understood Libby's intentions, until he understood himself better too. A baby was just about the worst thing that could happen to him—he'd never wanted children—and yet…even as he knew that to be true, there was something about this news that was punching him hard in the gut, making him fight for the child he'd never even wanted.

'And?' he asked, waiting with the appearance of patience.

Her eyes finally lifted, met his, and something jolted inside of his gut.

This was the mother of his child. They barely knew one another, yet here she was, standing in front of him with the face of an angel, telling him they'd made a baby together. A primal, fierce possessiveness fired in his blood.

'I never knew my dad,' she said, lips pulling to the side. 'I didn't even know his name.' Her brow crinkled as she contemplated that. 'I don't need you to be involved. I don't need you for anything,' she added, tilting her chin defiantly. 'But I did think you deserved to know. And our child will know about you too. Whatever capacity you choose to be in their life is up to you, and them, when they're old enough to decide.'

For the second time in as many minutes, the bottom fell out of his world.

It was a new sensation and he didn't like it at all.

She'd started the conversation with such uncertainty but, having made her pronouncement, she'd really taken the bull by the horns. Could she have any idea how deeply unsettling her description was to Raul?

Of course not. How could she?

He was being forced to grapple, at lightning speed, with something he hated the idea of yet now had to accept as reality. She was, on the one hand, offering him a way out. He could provide her with money so she could live comfortably and raise this baby without him.

But not wanting a child was not the same thing as being willing to ignore his own child, now that it was a reality rather than a theoretical scenario. The very idea was anathema to Raul, and he didn't have to be a psychotherapist to understand why.

No one had fought for him. No one had protected him. And no child of his would experience what he had—not while he had breath in his lungs.

'You are suggesting that you will raise the child by yourself?' He heard the derision in his voice and knew it was the wrong approach, but his emotions were moving beyond his control.

'Why not?' she asked, crossing her arms over her chest. His eyes dropped to her breasts before he could control the reaction. When he looked at her face once more he saw pink in her cheeks and something stirred in his groin.

He forced himself to hold her gaze. 'What will you do for money, Libby?' he pushed, waiting to see how she answered that. Did she see him as a meal ticket? If so, this was her chance.

Obviously, he intended to financially support his child, but it was strangely important to him to understand more about Libby. She was such an unknown quantity. She'd crashed into—and out of—his life in the most volatile, stunning way, so sometimes he'd wondered if he'd dreamed the whole encounter. They'd come together like magic and motion and then she'd left, and that had been that. The end. He knew nothing about her, and he wanted to. Not because of who she was as a woman, he told himself, but because she was to become the mother to his child.

'I've got some ideas,' she said, drawing his focus back to the conversation. 'I'm still working out the details, but don't worry,' she said with a hint of disdain. 'I'm not planning on taking a cent from you, Raul; this isn't a shakedown.'

He stared at her, embarrassed to have been seen through, and even more so because it made him seem ungenerous and irresponsible—he was neither. He'd hated the idea of Libby using him to secure some kind of payday, but it had never occurred to him *not* to contribute financially. The problem was, he wanted more than just to hand over cash every month.

'You need money,' he said, 'and obviously I will provide it.'

She closed her eyes, grimacing. 'I don't want that.'

'Why not?' he asked, fascinated by her response.

She lifted her slender shoulders in a shrug. 'I just… I know I can do this,' she said.

'You also know I am a very wealthy man,' he pushed, still trying to get her measure.

'Yes.'

'Do you imagine I would leave you here, struggling in squalor, raising a child I helped make?'

'I—' She looked around, her cheeks bright red now, and tears filmed her eyes. His gut twisted sharply with regret. Squalor might have been pushing it. Libby's apartment was down at heel but it was obvious she'd taken a lot of effort to make it bright and happy.

But this wasn't the time to backpedal. He had to make her see sense.

'I have never wanted children,' he said quietly.

She glanced at him, lips tight. 'You don't need to have anything to do with our baby—'

'That is no longer an option.'

Her eyes widened.

'I didn't plan this. I'm fastidious about protection for precisely this reason; I don't take any chances. Yet here we are.' He frowned, an idea occurring to him out of nowhere. An idea he hated with every part of himself and yet it formed with such clarity in his mind, he knew it was the only solution. His gut sank like a lead balloon. 'Are you absolutely certain about this?'

She spun away from him, reaching into a drawer and removing an envelope. She hesitated a moment, then slid it across to him. He took it, peeled the triangle back and removed a small, square picture. Grainy, but recognisable enough.

An ultrasound photo. His child. He stared at it, waiting to feel that magical emotion people talked about in moments such as this, waiting to feel a rush of love for the blurry, blob-like thing, but all he was conscious of was a need to move all the pieces into alignment so he could protect this child, as no one had protected him. That wasn't love, it was responsibility.

'I had a scan to confirm it,' she explained. 'I'm definitely pregnant. Sorry.'

He handed the picture back without looking at it again. 'It's not your fault.'

She winced. 'Still, it's not ideal.'

'No,' he agreed. 'It's far from it. But we can't change it now. So, let's make a plan.'

Let's make a plan.

Did he have any idea how comforting that statement was? Libby had spent the last two weeks feeling like she was going to be totally alone in this, and here was Raul, offering to take her hand in his, at least in terms of working out what to do next, and she could have wept with relief.

The feeling did not last long.

'I did not know my father either, Libby. Nor my mother. I have only a few very vague memories.' He frowned. 'You and I have one vital thing in common,' he said with steel in his voice. She waited, breath held, even as questions spawned in her mind about his up-bringing. 'We both know the particular insecurity that comes from a less than ideal childhood.'

She closed her eyes on a wave of recognition. Hadn't it been the first pledge she'd made to this baby, when she'd learned of their existence? That she would shield them from the pain and uncertainty she'd lived with?

'I will not allow history to repeat itself. Not for either of us.' His nostrils flared on the statement and she heard the determination in his tone.

'I feel the same way,' she murmured. 'It's why I wanted to tell you.'

'You wanted to give me the option of involvement,' he said, brushing past her acknowledgement, 'because your father and you didn't have that. But it's not enough, Libby. Not by a long shot.'

She pressed her back against the kitchen bench, needing strength. Her tea was tepid now; she took a sip anyway. 'What are you suggesting?'

Silence fell. The ticking of the clock took on an almost ominous tone.

'There is only one solution.' His voice was flat, devoid of all feeling and warmth. She stared at him, waiting for the penny to drop, because Libby could see no option beyond the one she'd suggested. Unless he intended to fight her for custody? She blanched at the very idea.

'Raul,' she mumbled. 'You can't mean to try to take the baby from me?' She trembled from head to foot. 'I know I don't have your resources, but I will do everything I can to be the best mother possible to our child. You can't—'

'That is not my intent.' He spoke quickly, immediately dismissing the idea.

She didn't feel the wave of relief she'd anticipated. She was on tenterhooks, waiting for him to say whatever was cogitating behind those intelligent eyes of his.

'I want to raise my child.'

Libby's heart stammered.

'I want to be in their life every day, not just occasionally, and I presume you feel the same way.'

She nodded, not trusting her voice to speak.

'Then the solution is obvious, and simple.' His tone was bland but she saw the look in his eyes. It was a look of sheer disbelief. 'We'll get married.'

Libby almost passed out. Her heart skipped a thousand beats and her eyes flashed with white.

'No.' She lifted a hand to her lips, pressing it there.

Something precious she'd nurtured inside of herself

since she was a girl was being strangled by his cold, pragmatic suggestion. The little girl who'd hidden in her room and read romantic fairy tales to escape the reality of her life, who'd promised herself that one day she'd make all her own fairy tales come true, had never given up on the idea of real, all-consuming love. Of finding the kind of man who was like a modern-day Prince Charming, who'd love her with all that he was, for all time. She'd hated the way her mother had gone through partners. It had made Libby all the more determined to believe in *true* love. In the idea of finding that one perfect person who was destined for her, and she'd been holding out for them all this time.

A cold marriage for the sake of a child, in the twenty-first century, was a death knell to all those hopes and dreams.

'I can't,' she whispered.

'Marriage is the last thing I want as well,' he responded, and hurt lashed her. She turned away from him then, looking out of the window and finding no pleasure remained in the view.

'We don't even know each other.'

'That's less important than being married before the baby arrives.' He spoke as though it were a foregone conclusion. 'You will be supported in every way,' he said, ignoring the fact she hadn't accepted his proposal. 'You will live in my home, have true financial stability and comfort. You will not have to work unless you want to— you can be a full-time mother, if that is your wish. This is not a jail sentence, but a gift of freedom. Our marriage can give you wings, can't you see that?'

'Marriage to a virtual stranger? Freedom?' she repeated, incredulous, turning to face him then wishing she hadn't when the sight of him made her central nervous system go into overdrive. Even now, feeling as she did, totally on edge and laced with panic, she was all too aware of him as a man, and that terrified her. 'How can you say that?'

'What will your life be like if you do not accept?'

'I'll manage,' she promised defiantly.

'And what about our child's life?' he pushed, moving closer, looking down at her with cool eyes, appraising her every gesture so she felt totally seen and vulnerable. 'Do you really think you can offer them enough?'

Her lips parted; it was a low blow. 'Of *course*.' But was she so sure of that? Hadn't it been the biggest problem she'd been trying to solve, since finding out she was pregnant? Her voice trembled. 'I will love this child enough to give them anything.'

'Evidently not,' he said quietly.

'What's that supposed to mean?'

'I am offering them everything—and you are choosing not to take it.'

Libby's eyes widened.

'This is not about you,' he continued, and shame curdled in her belly. 'I am not offering to marry you as a man offers for a woman. This is a sacrifice we would both be making, for the sake of our child. Is there any better reason to sacrifice, Libby?'

Did he have any idea how badly he was twisting the knife in her heart? Not because she felt anything for Raul, but because her longest-held dream was of being loved, really loved. On her loneliest nights, she'd consoled herself with visions of her future. Nothing special or glamorous—a very ordinary, happy life, in a nice simple cottage with a garden and an apple tree, a white timber fence with nasturtiums scrambling along it, sunlight dappling the thick, lush lawn, perfect for picnics, and most of all—love and laughter. Chubby little children whose hands would seek hers, and a husband who'd wrap his arms around her waist and draw her to him, their hearts in lockstep, always.

She expelled a soft sigh. It was a fantasy. A childish dream.

Maybe Raul was right… Maybe she needed to grow up and accept the reality of this. Fairy tales were for children; there were more important considerations here. In marrying Raul, Libby would be giving up on the idea of romantic love, of meeting her soulmate and losing her head to them. But there were other kinds of love that were just as important, and the love she already felt for her child, and knew they'd feel for her, was enough to start stitching her heart back together again. She could still know the contentment of a little hand in hers, of a toddler in her lap for reading time, of goodnight cuddles and kisses…all of the things she'd never had enough of.

Raul was right: marriage to him was a sacrifice, but she would make it, for the baby. But it would need to be the right kind of marriage, a partnership at least. If love wouldn't be part of the picture, she had to know there would at least be teamwork. They were going to be parents together, after all.

'Obviously, financially, you can offer us the world,' she said, running her hand over her stomach, pausing when his eyes followed the gesture and flared. Her heart trembled and when she spoke, her voice was unsteady. 'But I would need more, if I were to go along with this.'

His dark brows lifted, surprise showed in the depths of his grey eyes before he concealed it. 'What are your conditions?'

It was like he'd been expecting it, she thought, then realised he probably had. Raul Ortega was used to negotiations, and this was no different. He wasn't taking over a company now though, but her life, and she had to be just as pragmatic and sensible as he would be if their positions were reversed.

'I would want everything in writing before we got married,' she said, lips pulling to the side.

'A prenuptial agreement?' he prompted.

'Yes, exactly,' she agreed quickly. 'If something happened, and it might—we don't know each other well enough to just trust blindly—and our marriage ended, and even ended badly, I would need to know that I would continue to be…looked after. That our baby would be looked after.'

His nostrils flared and the look on his face showed how offended he was by her suggestion. Tone stiff, he said curtly, 'Naturally.'

'I beg your pardon, but it's not "natural",' she insisted. 'Plenty of women get the raw end of the deal, particularly in marriages like this—where one person enters into it with so much more.'

He crossed his arms over his chest. 'I will ensure you are taken care of, no matter what.'

She bit into her lower lip. 'It's not for my sake but the baby's,' she said, troubled by these negotiations even when she acknowledged their necessity. 'There should be a trust fund or something, set up for them. You don't know how you'll feel in five years, or ten, nor whom you might end up married to next and what they might ask you to do. I want this child's future to be inviolable if I do this.'

'A moment ago you were prepared to give up any claim whatsoever to my wealth,' he pointed out.

'Yes.' She nodded. 'But if I marry you, our baby will get used to living a certain way. I don't want him or her to have to face the prospect of losing that. Stability is important.'

'Fine.'

She couldn't tell if he believed her point was valid, but she took his agreement regardless.

'Describe what our marriage will be like,' she said after a beat, heat blooming in her cheeks.

'In what context?'

He was really going to make this awkward for her, wasn't he?

'Obviously, it won't be a real marriage, in the sense of…sex.' She stumbled over the last word in her statement. 'Contrary to whatever opinion you might have formed of me after that day, I'm not generally into meaningless encounters.'

A muscle throbbed in his jaw but otherwise he didn't react.

'You, on the other hand,' she continued a little breathily, 'presumably are.'

He lifted one thick dark brow and even though his expression didn't change she had the strangest feeling he was laughing at her.

'Go on.'

'I wouldn't expect that to change—' she sniffed '—but I would require your absolute discretion.'

His eyes narrowed almost imperceptibly.

'There are more kinds of insecurity than financial to worry about. I wouldn't want our child to suspect our marriage was anything other than...happy.'

'Fine.'

'To which end, we would both need to agree to treat one another with respect,' she said, thinking quickly. 'And to get to know one another well enough to be...' She searched for the right word.

'Friends?' he prompted, but his voice was loaded with cynicism.

'What's wrong with that?'

Raul looked at her for a long time, so long that Libby's chest felt as though it were going to explode from the pressure being exerted on her.

'We will get to know each other,' he said finally. 'Within reason.'

She frowned. 'What does that mean?'

'This is not an audition for a real marriage,' he said coldly. 'While we should be respectful and even *friendly*, it is important not to ever lose sight of why we are doing this. I will not fall in love with you, Libby, so please be realistic in your expectations. This is only for our child, okay?'

Her lips parted on a groundswell of shock. 'Wow, ego much?'

His eyes shuttered, concealing his feelings from her. 'I am simply being honest—which is, in my opinion, an important prerequisite for this.'

'Fine,' she agreed, knowing she should have been

grateful for his truthfulness, even when it cut her to the quick. It was just such a bald, frank assessment, another dropping of the guillotine on those childish hopes. But she wasn't stupid enough to put those dreams into Raul's hands, anyway! So what difference did it make if he was pronouncing they would always be loveless?

'I presume the same conditions imposed upon me would apply to you as well? If you were to take a lover, it would be with the utmost caution to avoid discovery.'

'Of course,' Libby said, rolling her eyes. 'But you really don't need to worry about that. I'm not exactly a highly sexed person,' she said, 'which makes the irony of this just all the more ridiculous.'

He was quiet. It was the only explanation for why Libby kept speaking, as if nervously filling the void.

'To think, the first time I have sex with anyone in three years I fall pregnant.' She groaned. 'I swear the fates are laughing at us, Raul.'

CHAPTER FIVE

HE TRIED NOT to wonder about that. He definitely didn't ask. But how could he fail to be curious about why a woman who was so sensual and passionate hadn't had sex in such a long time?

It was not the most important thing in that moment though, so he pushed it aside.

'Be that as it may,' he said with a tone of resignation. 'Here we are.'

'Yes, here we are.' She stared up at him, as if looking for an answer he didn't know how to give. An assurance. But he was all out of promises. Raul was moving into fresh new territory, and he wasn't going to pretend otherwise. 'Which brings me to my next point,' she said slowly.

'There's more?'

Libby rolled her eyes. 'We're talking about a marriage. Don't you think it's wise to go through more than a couple of details?'

She had a point, but Raul believed they would make it work however they had to. He knew all he needed on that score: they both cared about this child more than they did their own wishes. It was his only concern.

'What else?' he prompted.

'Where we'll live, for starters.'

'My headquarters are in New York.'

Her throat shifted as she swallowed. 'New York?' she said softly. 'For real?'

He scanned her features. 'You don't like it?'

'I've never been,' she replied. 'I've never been any-where. I can't just move to New York.'

'Why not? What's holding you here?'

She looked around.

'Do you have family? A support network?'

'I have friends,' she said, but weakly.

He expelled a breath. 'We can move back, if you don't like New York. For now, though, it's how it has to be. I cannot uproot my business at the drop of a hat and re-locate to Sydney.'

'You mean you don't want to,' she said stubbornly.

'I am prepared to make all sorts of accommodations for this child; I am asking you to meet me halfway.'

'New York is the other side of the world, that's not halfway.' Her expression was belligerent, but he could see she was waning on this point. 'I don't even have a passport.'

Raul's brows flexed as he processed her statement. It was totally antithetical to him—he who travelled at the drop of a hat, drawn to his business interests all over the world. But he could see the vulnerability in her face at having made the admission and didn't want to exac-erbate it.

'No problem. My assistant will arrange it.'

Libby's jaw dropped. 'Just like that?'

'You will likely have to fly to Canberra to expedite matters. Justine will arrange it.'

'Your assistant?'

'Yes.' He nodded once. 'Is there anything else?'

She shook her head, and she looked so lost, as though she was a little girl, stranded in a storm, that he felt the strangest compulsion to reach out and draw her into a hug, to stroke her back and promise her everything would be okay.

But Raul didn't really believe in those assurances.

He wanted, more than anything, to make their child's life perfect, but he wasn't stupid enough to promise any such thing. Life had a way of pulling the rug out from under you. It was better to brace for that, at all times, than live in a fool's paradise.

So he simply said, 'I'll see to the paperwork. You handle the passport. Deal?'

And, just like that, a week later, Libby was sitting on-board Raul's private jet, staring at a thick wad of papers, highlighter and pen in hand as though they were her sword and shield.

He'd engaged a law firm to advise her, but Libby wasn't going to leave things to chance. Trust didn't come easily for her, and she wasn't going to be stupid about something as important as her child's future.

So she sat, legs curled up beneath her on the enormous armchair, carefully reading the prenuptial agreement line by line, annotating where necessary, making notes of any queries she had.

The first few pages dealt expressly with the financial arrangements and custodial expectations. The amount Raul had suggested putting in trust for their child made Libby's eyes water. She felt a rush of compunction to imagine he thought she had any expectation of him setting aside quite so much. She'd simply meant *enough*. Enough for their child to never have to worry as she'd always worried. Enough to know they were financially secure, come what may.

Raul had made their unborn baby a multimillionaire even before they'd drawn breath.

By page five, they were onto a matter that made Libby blush for a whole other reason.

Extramarital considerations

She read the stipulations with a pulse that was thready and uneven.

It was everything they'd agreed, and then a little extra. In addition to the requirement that any extramarital relationships be kept completely discreet was the requirement that the spouse would be notified, to avoid potential awkwardness.

Libby couldn't believe she was actually contemplating signing a document like this. It made a mockery of everything she had ever believed about marriage!

'Good evening, ma'am.' A steward approached her, male, with blond hair and a broad smile. His accent was American. 'Would you care for some refreshments?'

Libby quickly shut the contract, mortified to think he might have seen even a hint of what was written on the page.

'Um…' she said, aware of not just the steward but also Raul. Though he sat further down the cabin, and she wasn't even looking at him, she felt his eyes on her. She knew he was watching.

Her pulse ratcheted up.

'I can bring you a menu,' he offered.

'Okay,' she agreed, fidgeting with her fingers. 'Thank you,' she added, forcing herself to smile.

Morning sickness, as pervasive and never-ending as it had been a few weeks ago, seemed to have given her a temporary reprieve and, if anything, Libby was hungry *all the time*. She found the cravings to be the strangest thing: she'd gone from enjoying reasonably simple foods to wanting to try things she'd never heard of. Inwardly, she couldn't help smiling as she imagined her baby's strong will already in evidence.

She stroked her stomach absentmindedly, staring out of the window at the jet-black sky as the plane cut its way across the globe.

A moment later, the steward was back, handing Libby a menu that was identical in branding to Raul's business card. She scanned it quickly, bypassing the savoury selection and landing instead on pancakes with bacon and a cup of tea.

'Won't take me long,' the steward said with another charming grin as he disappeared from the cabin.

Libby was not alone for long. Raul strode towards her, and every single one of Libby's senses went onto high alert as he took the seat opposite her, his long legs spread wide, his body the last word in relaxed athleticism. So why did his proximity have the opposite impact on her?

Every time they went a stretch without seeing one another, she forgot. She forgot how big and strong and *masculine* he was. How just being near him called to some ancient part of her, making her want to throw caution to the wind, just as she'd done on the boat. She'd put it down to the heat of the moment, the relief and the drama, but what was her excuse now?

Hormones?

She suppressed a grimace, turning to look out the window once more.

'How are you finding it?'

'Mortifying,' she answered honestly. 'I cannot believe you had a lawyer draft this.'

'Why?'

'Because it's so...*personal*,' she spluttered.

'They act for me in the strictest confidence,' he assured her. 'This document is completely private.'

'It's not that,' she said with a shake of her head. 'Doesn't it embarrass you that they think this is what our marriage is about?' She lifted the contract higher.

'It is what our marriage is about,' he said without a hint of shame. 'Besides which, I do not particularly care what my legal team thinks about my private life.'

Libby's eyes narrowed. 'I bet you don't care what anyone thinks,' she said, wishing on all the stars in the heaven that she knew just a little more about the man she was metaphorically getting into bed with.

'Not particularly,' he said with a shrug.

The steward returned with a cup of tea. Libby thanked him but made no effort to lift it off the table.

'It is my experience that people will generally think what they want whether you like their opinion or not. Worrying about it is therefore somewhat futile.'

Her lips twisted into the ghost of a smile. 'I suppose you're right,' she said, wondering at his innate confidence, and where it came from. Except it went beyond confidence. There was an air of such self-reliance that now Libby did wonder about his life, his childhood, his experiences. What had happened to shape him into the man he was today?

'You said you didn't really know your parents,' she murmured, placing the contract aside and giving him her full attention—or at least, finally showing that he already had it. 'Who raised you?'

Was she imagining the slight pause? The shift in his features?

'I was in foster care,' he responded crisply. It was an open-ended answer. She had no personal experience with the foster system, but she'd heard and read enough to know that some people didn't fare too well with it, while others did. She supposed it was down to the luck of the draw.

'And?'

His expression didn't change. 'And at fifteen, I ran away,' he said matter-of-factly. 'I decided I'd had enough of being parented, and wanted to take my chances on the streets.'

'You did?'

He nodded once.

'I can't even imagine…' she said softly.

He looked at her long and hard and Libby's mouth was suddenly as dry as dust.

'Can't you?'

Her eyes widened. How could he possibly know about her childhood?

'Why do I find that hard to believe?' he pushed.

She shook her head. 'I don't know.'

'Perhaps it's because I see something in you, Libby, something that is broken in all the same ways I was.' He ran his gaze over her features, slow and deliberate, as if he was tasting her. 'Am I wrong?'

Her lips parted. He wasn't wrong, but she'd always thought she hid her pain so well. She tried. Her childhood had been difficult, emotionally draining, hurtful. She carried those wounds to this day, yes, but Libby had sworn she wouldn't be defined by them. Where she felt pain, she acted with love. She smiled when her heart hurt. She was determined to respond to whatever darkness had been in her life with pure light. To hope for lasting love even when her mother had demonstrated again and again how unlikely that was.

That Raul had seen beyond her façade scared Libby to death.

'I don't think we'd be entering into this marriage if we hadn't both experienced a rough start to life,' she said uneasily.

'Which means?'

He was asking for specifics and Libby knew it was only fair that she should give them. After all, he had. At least, a brief enough outline for her to gain more of an understanding of him.

'My mother was single,' Libby said, sipping her tea, forcing herself to meet Raul's eyes. 'Except when she wasn't. The only thing is, she never met a man she wanted to be with for more than a few months.' Libby rushed through the explanation. 'I had a lot of stepdads,' she added with a grimace.

Raul was very still across from her, his eyes glittering when they met hers with a hardness that took her breath away. 'It takes a lot more than biology to be a good parent.'

She nodded her agreement. She'd seen that first-hand.

'Libby.' His voice was gruff, deep. 'What we're doing here, *this* is who we are. We will do right by our child, in a way no one ever did for us.' The determination in his voice, the pride, took her breath away.

Tears sparkled on her lashes as she nodded, not sure she could trust her voice to speak.

'This is all that matters,' he said quietly.

Libby knew then that they'd made the right decision. This was all about their baby, and always would be.

He had been careful not to touch her as they entered the lift to his penthouse. He'd been careful not to touch her since collecting her from her place in Sydney, and a strange swelling of something had begun to stretch in his chest.

Protectiveness.

It was the sight of Libby with her bashed-up old suitcase and a look in her eyes that was pure determination and strength. As if to say, 'Show me everything you've got; I'm ready for it.'

She was a fighter. He recognised that quality; he understood it. He didn't doubt she could take care of herself, and their child.

But she didn't have to.

Raul hadn't wanted this. It was the antithesis of what he wanted, in fact, and yet here he was, ready to protect the mother of his child with his life.

Despite her air of strength, he felt her nervousness, her anxieties about the step she was taking away from the familiar, and he'd wanted to reach across and put a hand on her knee as the car had pulled out from the kerb.

But he hadn't.

Just as he hadn't put his hand in the small of her back to guide her up the stairs when they'd reached his plane. Nor had he reached out and placed his hand over hers when they'd spoken on the plane and realised how similar their goal was, to protect their child from the sort of childhood they'd had. But he'd wanted to.

The longer he'd sat opposite Libby, watching as she flicked through the document and then fell asleep, highlighter with the lid off, small body curled up in the too-big armchair—they'd never felt too big for him—his fingers had tingled with a want to simply feel. Just one stroke of her soft cheek, to remind himself…to remember.

The air in the lift hummed with a sultry, seductive pulse, urging him to move closer to her. To brush against her, almost as if by accident. But there was a warning there too, because he suspected whatever incendiary spark had flared between them on the boat was still ignited, and they'd be all kinds of stupid to let it burn out of control.

If there wasn't a child involved.

If they weren't getting married.

But this was a serious, lifelong commitment to do right by their infant. He wouldn't let biological impulses complicate everything, so he stood firm on the other side of the lift, staring straight ahead, barely breathing until the doors opened and he waited for the release of the pent-up tension, the energy.

The relief didn't come.

Grinding his teeth, he stood at the doors to the lift,

holding his hand across them and waiting for Libby to precede him.

Her eyes flashed nervously to his then looked straight ahead.

'Oh,' she murmured, lips parting.

The lift opened directly into the foyer of his apartment—a large space that was decorated as it had been when he'd bought the place, all in beige and white, with a big mirror above a hallstand that had a decorative bowl and nothing else.

Raul lived a minimalistic life, despite his wealth. He'd learned as a teenager to need only a few small things, to be ready to leave at any point. He hadn't consciously kept that habit but, now that he thought about it, he had very little connection to anything in his apartment. There were only a few things in here he'd want to take if he left. Which was why it had been easy to buy the place and keep it basically as it had been.

'You can change anything you don't like,' he said, stepping out into the foyer and placing his keys and wallet in the bowl, then turning back to her. But Libby had already stepped away from him, was moving deeper into the penthouse, one hand lifted to her lips as she stared at the double height room beyond the foyer. He tried to see it through her eyes. Through the eyes of the teenager he'd once been, so poor he hadn't eaten for days, sleeping in an alleyway that reeked of urine and sweat.

It was magnificent, objectively speaking. The penthouse had been made of two full storeys of apartments, combined by the previous owners. The floor-to-ceiling windows offered panoramic views of Manhattan, and there was a deep balcony with a spa beyond the kitchen.

'We can't raise a baby here,' she said, turning to look at him, and instead of there being admiration in her features, he registered abject horror.

He frowned. 'You don't like it?'

She looked around again, as if she might see something else in the apartment she'd missed on first inspection. 'It's not that.' She shook her head. 'It's…just…so…'

He waited, curious as to what word she would choose.

'A baby couldn't relax here,' she said then laughed softly, nervously. 'I couldn't relax here. My God, Raul, this is—' She bit down nervously on her lower lip, and that same protective urge fired in his gut. To hell with it.

He closed the distance between them and put his hand on her upper arm. A gesture designed purely to reassure and comfort, nothing more, and yet damn it if his fingertips didn't spark the second he touched her. She expelled a sharp breath and her eyes lifted to his, so he felt the world tipping sideways in a way he immediately wanted to fight.

'It's just a place to live.'

'But it's not a home,' she said urgently, swallowing, and he felt her tremble like a little bird. His gut twisted. What did he know about home? He'd never had one. 'Not like I've always wanted to raise a child in.'

Raul had bought the place because it was a good investment and he could afford it. A divorce had meant it was being sold for under market value; he acted quickly to secure it and he hadn't regretted the purchase since. But he had no emotional ties to the place.

'Okay, we'll find somewhere else.'

Her laugh now was a little manic. 'Just like that?'

'Why not?'

Libby shook her head, wrapping her arms around her torso. He didn't drop his hand. He hoped his touch was reassuring to her in some way, even when it was unsettling to him. 'It's fine. I'll get used to it.'

But Raul didn't like the tone of her voice—anxious and concerned. His thumb stroked her arm gently. 'Hey.' He drew her face to his. She stared up at him, eyes wide, looking for something in the depths of his expression, but he didn't know what. 'We will make this work.'

It was a promise he made to the both of them, something they both needed in that moment, to hear, and believe.

CHAPTER SIX

A WEEK AFTER moving to New York, Libby had to admit her fears had been baseless. Her worries about how she and Raul would make this work, her concern that their sexual chemistry would make any kind of cohabiting situation untenable, had evaporated in the face of the fact they barely saw one another.

Raul worked long hours. So long she had begun to wonder how he functioned—even to worry a little, because how could a person sustain themselves when working so hard? And when he was home, or rather in the sky palace, as she'd started thinking of it, it was more than large enough to accommodate the pair of them without them needing to interact. Libby had her own spacious bedroom, balcony and bathroom, and she tended to eat dinner alone, hours before Raul returned. Her days were long and solitary, but Libby refused to give into the temptation to feel sorry for herself.

While this was far from her ideal situation, there was plenty to be thankful for, and excited about. She focused on the baby and on exploring this enormous, exciting city. She certainly didn't think about the dreams she'd always cherished, and about how far her arrangement with Raul was from the safety and security of the real, loving marriage she'd wanted since she was a little girl.

Raul's apartment was on the Upper East Side, and Libby discovered she was an easy stroll from many of the sights she'd seen in movies and on TV. From famous restaurants and grocery stores to museums, galleries, Central Park, and just the streets themselves, she kept herself busy by walking for miles and miles each day. It was admittedly far colder than Libby had ever thought possible, and frequently she'd been caught out in the snow, but on the first day in town she'd found a department store and bought a discount puffer coat that zipped up from the knees to the collar. It was like wearing a blanket, and when combined with gloves and a beanie, she was warm enough to walk and walk.

It made her tired though—pregnancy was exhausting, anyway—but she was always glad to be tuckered out at the end of the day and ready to flop into bed. Sleep came easily most of the time, meaning she didn't lie awake, staring at the ceiling, wondering about Raul, and this bizarre arrangement of theirs.

And so one morning, eight days after arriving in America, Libby woke and looked out at the crisp blue sky and contemplated which direction she'd strike out in, where she might go, what she might see. She didn't think about Raul, she didn't think about their baby, she just focused on keeping herself busy, day by day, until one day, this all felt normal.

She made herself a piece of toast for breakfast, eyeing her Vegemite jar with a hint of concern. It was already half empty.

'Morning.'

Libby startled, almost dropping her tea into the sink, as her gaze jerked across the room to find Raul standing there, arms crossed, legs wide, watching her.

Her mouth went dry and her heart began to pound; her lips parted on a quick sigh. The temptation to cross the room and touch him was totally unwelcome. She mentally planted her feet to the ground, refusing to surrender to the sudden desire.

'Hi,' she said unevenly. 'What are you doing here?'

His expression was quizzical. 'In my home?'

She rolled her eyes. 'You know what I mean.' Forcing herself to act normal, or try to seem normal, she lifted a piece of toast to her lips, took a small bite, chewed, struggled to swallow. 'You're usually long gone by now.'

His eyes flickered over her face. 'We have to sign the paperwork,' he said, reaching for the tie that was hanging loose either side of his chest and beginning to draw it together. His fingers were nimble and deft, working the silk until it formed a perfect knot at his throat. She was transfixed by the simple, mechanical gesture. He obviously performed the task often, and yet there was something about his confident motions that made her skin lift in goosebumps.

'Oh.' Libby's heart thudded against her chest. 'Now?'

'As soon as possible. Have your lawyers looked it over?'

She shook her head, took another bite of toast to buy time, aiming for casual nonchalance. 'I wanted to read it through first.'

He looked at her expectantly.

'I'll do it today,' she promised, looking longingly towards the outside world, thinking of the walk she'd been planning on.

'Okay. Let's discuss it tonight. Dinner?'

Libby's eyes strayed back to Raul's face, surprise in her features. 'Oh.' She dusted crumbs from the side of her lips. 'I mean... Sure,' she heard herself agree, even when inwardly she wanted to run from the idea of dinner with Raul, discussing the contract for their marriage.

But wasn't she the one who'd insisted on all of this?

On a proper prenuptial agreement, on them trying to form a relationship that had some kind of semblance to civility and friendship? They couldn't do that by never being in the same room.

'Okay,' she said with more confidence. 'I'll cook.'

He looked as though she'd suggested an afternoon skydive. 'Please don't bother. I'll organise something.'

'It's no trouble,' Libby promised. 'I like to cook, really.'

'It wasn't my intention to put you out.'

Libby expelled a breath and then laughed unsteadily. 'Raul, if we're going to do this, we have to start acting more normally. We're going to be raising a child together. I'm going to cook meals—I *like* to cook. It isn't a big deal.'

He nodded slowly, still looking far from convinced. 'If you're sure.'

'I am.' She felt strange. This was the closest they'd come to normal domesticity—him here, in the mornings, putting on a tie, talking about something they needed to do together, planning for dinner.

'Any food allergies?' she asked as he reached for his jacket and pulled it on.

Raul's laugh was a single bark, but it spread through her body like wildfire and then she was grinning too. This man probably had the constitution of a lion. 'I like food,' he said, walking to the door. 'All food, and lots of it.'

'Got it,' she murmured, taking another bite of toast. 'Make loads.'

He shot her a smile as he opened the door and her heart jettisoned from her chest and into her throat. Something like panic slicked her palms. 'See you tonight, Libby.'

By the time Libby had made her way to the amazing grocery store on the west side of the park and perused the aisles and deli counter, decided what she was going to make then bought the ingredients, she was too laden to make it home on foot, so she had her first experience of a New York City cab—which she loved, and she and the driver made conversation the whole way around the park and up Fifth Avenue. She paid with cash and her dwindling supply put her in mind of how pressing her financial situation was. She knew it was a conversation she had to have with Raul.

After all, she had no employment prospects in New York as she wasn't legally able to work, and there was still rent to cover on her apartment back home. She'd made the decision to continue her tenancy, because it seemed too permanent to get rid of the flat just yet. She wasn't ready.

But the walls were closing in on her. She felt the financial insecurity pinching her, just as it always had as a child. Since leaving school, she'd been determined to stand on her own two feet. To work just as hard as she could to make sure she'd never have to worry about money ever again. Yet here she was, in a gilded cage, without her own financial security, and it scared her, even when she knew somehow that Raul would never see her go hungry. That wasn't quite the same thing as being in control of your own financial destiny, but there was nothing she could do about that for now. Once the baby was born she'd make it a priority to find a way to stand—at least a little—on her own.

Back in the apartment, she set dinner cooking then made a tea and sat down with the contracts, opening them to the last page she'd read on the flight over, and flushed to the roots of her hair.

To see the intimate details of their marriage written in such stark detail did something funny to her pulse, just as it had on the plane. She knew she should be glad that it was all there in black and white, but she couldn't help the hot flush that ran over her skin as she contemplated the sort of marriage they were negotiating, that two teams of lawyers would be aware of.

It all just felt so…depressing.

She sighed, turning the page, focusing on the next section. Schooling. She read with interest the provisions laid out by Raul—all very reasonable. They were to have equal say in the choice of school, and where they could not find agreement he'd selected a family counselling service to offer mediation. Libby turned the page, continued to read.

The next heading was: *In the Event of Both Parents' Deaths*. She blanched a little, the thought one that hadn't occurred to her. Her grip on the pen tightened, because the all-consuming love she already felt for their unborn child made her reticent to even contemplate such an event—the idea of their baby being flotsam in the world, with no one to love him or her, filled her with despair.

In preparation for the unlikely event of both parents' deaths, a suitable guardian will be nominated and agreed upon by both parents prior to the child's birth.

Libby's heart stammered. A suitable guardian?

She felt queasy at the idea of not being able to raise her own child, but of course it was something to consider, an important point to tick off. It wasn't likely to come to pass but, given Raul's upbringing, it made sense he'd want to know they'd made an effort to mitigate any eventuality.

She turned the page quickly: *In the Event of Divorce.*

And there it was, in black and white. The reality of what they'd do if their shotgun marriage failed. Heart thumping, she skimmed the page first, then returned to the top and read it properly.

The document set out terms requiring them to live no more than three miles apart, to share custody fifty per cent per parent, and to mutually agree to any other caretaking arrangements. It was all very reasonable. So reasonable that, for a brief moment, Libby contemplated taking the deal.

After all, they were terms she could almost live with.

Almost, but not quite.

Sharing her baby? Not having them with her half of the time, but rather sending them to live with Raul. She shuddered. Perhaps there would come a point when she'd be prepared for that, but it was not now, not yet. Not before they'd even given this a proper try.

She pushed the contracts aside and returned to the

kitchen, trying not to think about the contingencies they were making a plan for. All Libby wanted to focus on was her baby.

'Where did you learn to cook?' he asked, shovelling a third serving of lamb onto his plate along with mashed chickpeas and some greens. Libby stared at him, aghast. It had been delicious and tender, but surely he'd had enough?

'Um…' she said, momentarily not computing his question because she was so caught up in his appetite. 'I suppose I cooked a lot, growing up.'

He waited for her to continue, lifting a fork of dinner to his lips. She was mesmerised. Not just by his appetite but by everything about him. The entire experience of having him come home from work, place his leather laptop bag down on a kitchen stool, drape his jacket nearby, roll up his shirtsleeves to reveal two tanned forearms, remove his tie, flick open his shirt… It had all been so… intimate.

She glanced away from him, the word catching her by surprise.

They were *not* intimate. They'd slept together once, and they were having a baby, but there was nothing close nor personal about their dynamic, even when they were sitting opposite one another, sharing a meal.

'As a hobby?' he asked, though there was something in the depths of his grey eyes that showed he perceived more than he was revealing. That he already suspected the answer to that question.

She shook her head slowly. 'It was one of my jobs.'

He was quiet as he contemplated that. 'One of?'

'I helped run the house,' she said, pressing her fork around her plate, manoeuvring a piece of broccolini from one side to the other. 'My mother wasn't much for house-work, but she expected things to be just so. She liked nice food, said it was our job to provide a good meal for the man of the house.' Libby couldn't help rolling her eyes. 'She was old-fashioned like that.'

Raul made a noise of disapproval.

'Besides which, I like food too, and it was either learn to cook or eat very badly, so I learned.'

'How?'

'I watched tutorials on the internet,' she said. 'I had to get creative. We couldn't afford a lot of the ingredients, so I'd take a meal and work out how I could do some-thing similar for a fraction of the cost. There was a lot of pasta and rice substitution,' she said with a tight smile.

Raul's eyes narrowed; sympathy softened the edges of his mouth.

She cleared her throat. 'But I liked it,' she said, be-cause the last thing she wanted was for him to feel sorry for her. 'I got a sense of satisfaction out of what I could make. I enjoyed shopping, preparing, and discovering that whatever I'd cooked was actually pretty damned good. Most of the time.' She wrinkled her nose. 'There were also some disasters.'

His laugh was soft, warming. She liked the sound of it.

'When did you move out?' he asked, eyes heavy on her face.

'My mother left me, actually,' Libby said. 'I was nine-teen. She'd started living with a new guy a few months before. He got a job in Brisbane, and I came home from work one day to find the place empty except for my bed.'

'Charming,' Raul muttered.

Libby made a sound of agreement. 'I was an adult.' She shrugged, trying not to focus on the feeling of betrayal and hurt. 'It's not like I was too young to manage. I coped.' Her chin tilted and she felt the look in his eyes, the emotions there, and wished he'd stop looking at her with so much pity, or something.

'How did you cope?'

'I was already working,' she pointed out. 'I just had to find somewhere smaller, cheaper, work a bit more.'

He made another noise. 'Always as a cleaner?'

'Actually,' she said wistfully, 'I got a job as a kitchen hand at first. I had big dreams of applying for an apprenticeship, becoming a chef.'

'Why didn't you?'

'I couldn't afford it,' she said with a shake of her head.

'The degree?'

'No. The apprentice salary was so low, and I wouldn't have been able to work as many hours and study. It just wasn't tenable. I always told myself "one day", but then life just gets away from you sometimes, doesn't it?' she remarked quietly. 'I'm twenty-six years old. It was just a pipedream, anyway.'

His brows drew together and Libby shook her head.

'Please stop looking at me like that.'

'Like what?'

'As though you feel sorry for me. I hate it.'

Surprise showed on his face for a moment, before he contained it. 'I think you got the raw end of the deal,' he said after a beat.

'But so do lots of people. I'm happy, Raul. Really,

I am. I like my life and I liked my job. It's not what I dreamed of, but I make it work.'

'I'm sure you do.' His voice and expression were now even more unsettling than the pity he'd shown a moment earlier, because Libby heard admiration in his tone and it pulled at something deep inside her, something she preferred to keep locked away completely. 'Is your mother still in Brisbane?'

Libby shook her head. 'She passed away a few years ago.'

Raul's eyes glittered as he waited for Libby to express an answering emotion to that statement.

'I was sad I didn't get to see her again, before she died. I often wondered if she regretted...well, lots of things,' Libby said with a humourless smile. 'I wonder, sometimes, if she missed me.'

'Your mother sounds like a selfish woman.'

It was a fair assessment. 'In many ways, yes, she was.'

'It's unlikely that someone like her is capable of feeling regret. I'm sorry.'

Libby laughed then, a soft sound of surprise. 'Don't be. I appreciate honesty.'

'I know you do,' he said quietly, then, to lighten the mood, pointed to his plate. 'This is honestly one of the best meals I've ever eaten. Thank you for making it for me, Libby.'

Warm pleasure flooded her veins and Libby smiled across at him, already wondering what she might cook next. But that was a silly thought. A red herring. They weren't a couple, and this wasn't the beginning of some kind of happy domestic relationship. It was nothing like the dreams she'd cherished—where she'd meet someone who swept her off her feet for real, not like her mother's silly, unstable relationships.

Despite the fact Raul was charming and Libby had enjoyed sharing a meal with him, she knew she couldn't lose sight of what they were doing.

It wasn't until Raul had cleared the table, and Libby had made some hot drinks and put out a tray of biscuits, that they got around to discussing the finer points of the contract. Libby was quick to admit to Raul how thorough he'd been.

'It's what I do,' he said, dismissing her praise.

'Write contracts?' she asked, curling her legs up beneath her on the sofa, one hand wrapped around her cup of tea.

'Make agreements,' he clarified, tapping his pen against the papers. 'Did you want to make any changes?'

She shook her head. 'I haven't sent it to the lawyers you hired for me yet. I don't really see that I need to.'

'You should,' Raul murmured. 'For additional protection.'

'From you?' she asked, genuinely surprised.

He nodded. 'It's always a good idea to get outside advice.'

'It seems pretty simple to me, but okay. I'll email it tonight.'

His eyes met hers, holding, appraising. 'We should discuss dates.'

Libby's first thought was a misunderstanding. She thought for a moment he was implying they should *go* on a date, in a romantic sense, and everything got wonky and strange, before sanity reasserted itself and she re-alised he meant the dates on a calendar. 'For what?'

'The wedding,' he said. 'I thought, given the practical nature of our marriage, we could go to a registry office for the wedding itself. But you may have other ideas.'

'I—' Libby stared at him, the wedding something she'd given startlingly little thought to. 'No, a registry office is fine by me too. Why dress up what we're doing?' she added. 'It's little more than a contractual agreement, right?'

'Yes,' he responded, scanning her face. 'That bothers you?'

Libby's eyes widened. She didn't bother to deny it, but nor did she want to admit how *much* the nature of this marriage bothered her. What she'd wanted for herself no longer mattered; she was going to become a mother. This baby would always come first for Libby. 'It's just… I know so little about you,' she said after a beat. 'To be getting married to a virtual stranger, having a baby with him…it's a lot.'

He appeared to relax back in his chair. 'What would you like to know?'

She laughed at the unexpectedness of that, and his grin pulled at her belly. She looked away, sipping her tea. 'Where are you from?'

'Spain.'

'More specifically?'

'Madrid.'

'When did you leave?'

'When I was twenty-one.'

'Do you ever go back?'

'Yes.'

'Often?'

'As required.'

She rolled her eyes. He was answering her questions but it felt a little like pulling teeth. She persisted.

'Do you ever want to live there again?'

His shrug was indolent. 'Who knows?'

She laughed despite herself.

'That's funny?'

'You don't strike me as a free spirit.'

He grinned. 'I go where I need to.'

'What constitutes need?'

'Work,' he said immediately, sipping his coffee.

'So that's what brought you to New York?'

'Yes.'

'Why New York?'

'The first global company I acquired was based here. I bought the building with the company. It just made sense.'

Her eyes widened. 'The whole building?'

His smile was slow to spread. 'Yes.'

'Just how rich are you, Raul?'

His laugh was low and gruff. 'I've lost count.'

'Whereas I have spent the last however many years knowing down to the last cent what's in my bank account,' she volleyed back with a small shake of her head.

'Speaking of which—' He stood, moving to the kitchen, where his jacket had been discarded, and removed his wallet. He walked towards her. 'This is for you.'

She took what he was offering without looking, but when she drew the item closer, she saw it was a credit card, with her name on it.

'Oh.' Her cheeks flushed. She wished she could say she didn't need it, that she could decline, but the reality was, she would need his financial support. That was part of the deal they'd made.

'What's wrong?' he asked, crouching down in front of her, staring at her in that way he had, as if unpicking every little piece of her.

'It's just… I've worked and earned for a long time. It's going to take some getting used to, just accepting money from you.'

'I respect that,' he murmured. 'This can be temporary, Libby. Once the baby is born, when you're ready, you can go back to work, or study, whatever you'd like. Don't overthink it.' He reached out then, almost as if against his judgement, and put a hand on her knee. 'We both know I can afford it.'

Libby's heart raced as she placed the credit card on the end table and forced a smile to her face. It would be different if they were in a real relationship, a real marriage. Then she'd have no trouble considering whatever was Raul's to be hers, and vice versa—such as it was.

'You'll need to come by the bank to sign some papers this week—to do with the trust funds I've set up.'

'Oh, when shall we go?' she asked, factoring that into her busy schedule of wandering the streets.

'You won't need me,' he said, standing and returning to his own seat. 'Justine can schedule it at your convenience.'

'Great,' she said, over-bright, feeling like a fool for expecting him to accompany her. Silence fell, but it was a heavy silence, at least, for Libby. She was aware of too much. Of what she'd learned about Raul and what she still didn't know, of the disparity in their finances and general life experiences and, most of all, her awareness of him as a man, which was making it hard to think with the objectivity she suspected she needed.

'I have also made enquiries about an obstetrics team,' he said, leaning forward, elbows resting on his thighs.

Libby's mouth formed a perfect O. 'You have?'

'You're pregnant, remember?' he drawled, face deadpan, but she smiled anyway.

'That's right, I'd forgotten,' she joked, patting her stomach. In the last couple of days she'd *felt* different, a little softer, and her jeans had become harder to button up, so she'd taken to wearing them with just the zip in place. 'But isn't there just a local hospital or something I can go to?'

'This is better.'

Libby dipped her head to hide a smile. She wasn't about to argue. If he wanted to pay for the best medical care money could buy, who was she to disagree? But...

'A whole obstetrics team?' she said after a beat, recollecting his phrasing.

'A nurse, midwife, two obstetricians—'

'Two?'

'In case one is unavailable.'

She laughed. 'Raul, we have no reason to think there are going to be any complications with my delivery. I'm young and healthy.'

'Nonetheless, why take chances?'

'Okay,' she said softly. 'We'll do it your way.'

'Thank you,' he said, and Libby's eyes lifted to his face at the unexpected expression of gratitude.

Was this how it would be between them? Discussion,

agreement, compromise, gratitude? It wasn't a happily-ever-after love match, but it still felt pretty heartwarming for someone like Libby, who'd never known the pleasure that could come from mutual respect.

She returned his smile, even as she kept a firm grip on her heart and mind. He was charming, but she wouldn't allow herself to be charmed. 'You're welcome.'

CHAPTER SEVEN

RAUL KNEW SHE was pregnant. He believed her. He'd seen the sonogram image for himself. And yet, being here in the obstetrics clinic with a wand pressed to Libby's stomach and a gloopy grey and white image on the screen, listening to the sound of their baby's heartbeat in the air, Raul found it almost impossible to breathe. He stared at the screen—their baby—and was suddenly on the verge of a panic attack.

At least, he presumed it to be that—he'd never known this feeling before.

His vision filled with white and his lungs burned as though he'd run a marathon. And inside his mind he shouted every curse word he knew.

How the hell could he do this?

He couldn't be a father. He couldn't be a parent. What the hell did he know about raising someone? About taking care of another person? He'd made it his mission in life to care only for himself, to keep everyone else at a distance, and now he was looking at a tiny little life that would be *his*. His responsibility, his burden, his duty, his to care for and nurture and influence.

He swallowed, desperately needing moisture to return to his mouth and breath to reinflate his lungs.

'Raul?' Libby was looking up at him, her face showing concern. 'Are you okay?'

He tried to smile but suspected it was more of a grimace. Libby blinked, but not before he'd seen the hurt in her eyes.

He was messing everything up. He reached down and squeezed her hand, her need for reassurance in that moment trumping everything else. She didn't look up at him; her attention was focused on the screen.

He was ruining everything. God, he needed to pull himself together.

'Well?' He spoke more curtly than he'd intended. 'Is the baby healthy?'

The doctor's smile was practised. 'Everything here looks fine,' he assured them. 'I can see arms, legs, a heart.' He pulled the wand away from Libby's stomach. 'We'll do another scan in a few weeks.'

'Why?' Raul asked swiftly. 'Do you suspect something's wrong?'

'No,' the obstetrician said, running a hand through his hair. 'It's standard procedure, to investigate the organs. Today, we'll take some bloods, run a few more tests, but I haven't seen anything that concerns me.'

The obstetrician handed Libby a paper towel, which she used to wipe her belly, then she gingerly replaced her shirt. Raul's eyes clung to her stomach, the soft roundedness there hinting at what was to come, and something stole over him, a tingling sensation in the pit of his gut that ran like waves through his whole body.

Almost as soon as she'd told him about the baby he'd felt a primal rush of connection, a need to protect and provide for, and he felt that again now. This was *his* baby.

Libby was to be *his* wife. Only he had no idea how to be a husband or a father. He had no idea how to be anything to anyone. He hated the thought of being relied on, even as he knew it had to be this way. But inside, Raul felt as though he was drowning; he wanted, for the first time in his life, to run as far away as he could from a challenge.

Libby desperately didn't want to take it personally, but the hour spent in the obstetrician's office had been one of the most emotionally complex of her life. On the one hand, there was the rush of hearing their baby's heartbeat, of seeing the little person on screen once more, of being reassured by the obstetrician that everything was developing as it should be. These things made Libby's heart warm and her soul glow. But then there was Raul, who'd spent the entire appointment looking as though he was being dragged through the very fires of hell, who'd made it obvious at every point that he didn't want to be there.

So why had he even come?

They left the health clinic with her nervous system rioting. She took several deep breaths, told herself to calm down, that it didn't matter what Raul felt or thought, that they were having an unplanned baby and naturally it was a complicated thing for each of them to navigate. But at the same time, she was angry. Angry in a way that fired the blood in her veins and made her temperature soar, angry in a way that put pink in her cheeks and caused her hands to tremble, so when they reached his car he asked, 'Are you okay?'

Libby shot him a look, contemplated answering honestly, but instead responded with, 'Why wouldn't I be?'

He frowned, unconvinced, but didn't say anything else. They rode back to his apartment in silence, with Libby looking out of the window, waiting for a sense of calm that didn't come.

He spoke once they entered the lift. 'Libby.'

She didn't look at him.

'What's going on?'

She expelled a shaky breath. 'Nothing.'

'Obviously that's not true.'

The doors pinged open into his apartment. She stepped inside, removing her shoes before moving through to the palatial living area. It was so exquisitely beautiful and, for some reason, it was the stunning opulence of the room that made her reach tipping point, and suddenly, her eyes sparkled with unshed tears.

'Libby?' His voice was a growl. She clung to her anger, rather than the swamping sensation of sadness threatening to devour her. But when she thought of what this experience was supposed to be like, what it would have been like if she were going through this with a true partner, she was thrown into a state of despair that was totally uncharacteristic for her.

'It's nothing,' she said as a tear slid down her cheek.

He was quiet. Perhaps if he'd pushed her again, she would have clammed up, refused to speak, but the palpating silence dragged words from her almost against her will.

'I wish you hadn't come,' she said quietly, and with relief, because it felt good to be honest with him.

Raul was very still, his expression impassive. 'To the appointment just now?'

She nodded. 'You couldn't have made it any plainer

how much you didn't want to be there, how miserable you are about this whole thing. And I get it. You didn't want this, but it's happening, we're having a baby, and I don't want to be made to feel as though I'm ruining your life. Especially not in moments like that, when I should be able to just enjoy the experience.' She sucked in a breath, on a roll now. 'This isn't what I wanted for my life either, you know, but we're having a baby, and even when the circumstances aren't ideal, I'm still excited, I still want to make the most of each day of this pregnancy.' She angled her face away, unable to meet his eyes any more.

'You're right.' His admission surprised her. 'I didn't handle that well.'

She bit into her lip. 'You just shouldn't come to any more appointments.'

'That's not what I want.'

'Yeah, and I don't want to feel like I'm ruining your life,' she repeated, turning back to face him. 'It's not fair.'

'No, it's not.' He was quiet, still, and she felt like he was going to say something, but a moment later he nodded. 'If you don't want me there again, I won't come.'

Libby's heart did a strange, convulsive twist. The moment he said it, she realised it was the opposite of what she actually wanted: Raul by her side, *happy* about the baby. How unrealistic and pathetic! No matter how hard she tried, the optimist in Libby was struggling to accept the limitations of their arrangement. But she knew she had to, for her own sake. It was the only way she could do this.

Raul moved towards the lift with a steady gait, pausing once he'd pressed the button and the doors had pinged open. 'I'll see you tonight.'

Libby turned away from him, closing her eyes on a wave of sadness, and remorse. She wished now that she hadn't said anything. It had been futile and unnecessary. He was entitled to his feelings, just as she was hers.

But a moment later she heard footsteps and realised he hadn't left.

'This is hard for me,' he said, and when she turned to look at him, his features bore a mask of tension. She swallowed past a lump in her throat. 'I didn't know my parents. I did not have a good experience in the foster system. The streets were... You can imagine.' He ran a hand over the back of his neck, the action drawing her attention to the tightness in his frame. 'I have been alone a long time. I thought I would always be alone.' He paused, eyes boring into hers. 'I have no idea how to do any of this.' He gestured from himself to Libby. 'I panicked today.'

His raw honesty made her feel something she hadn't expected, something softening in her core. She didn't know why, but she nodded slowly, and he took that as encouragement or a prompt to continue, because he said, 'I am used to knowing exactly how to do what I need, in every situation. I am used to being in control, to running all aspects of my life.'

Libby expelled a soft breath. 'You can't control this,' she said gently. 'I get it; that's scary.'

A muscle throbbed in his jaw. 'I felt good things today too, Libby. Seeing our baby, hearing their heart beating.' He pressed a hand to his chest. 'I felt it. I just... didn't want to.'

More tears sparkled on Libby's lashes, but these were tears of relief.

'You have not ruined my life.'

She closed her eyes, surprised by how badly she needed to hear that, and by how much she wanted to understand Raul and his reactions.

'I'm sorry I got mad with you,' she said gently. 'I was scared too.'

His brows drew together, and she thought he might have been about to reject her assessment, but then he moved closer, pressing his thumb to her chin, tilting her face towards his. 'You're going to be a great mother.'

She blinked up at him, heart in her throat. 'How do you know?'

'Look at what you're already doing for our baby,' he said, stroking her cheek. Libby's stomach twisted. Did he understand how much she wanted this reassurance? To believe she'd be different to her own selfish mother? 'I'm sorry I upset you,' he said. 'I was thoughtless.'

She shook her head, silently denying his statement. 'This is unchartered territory for both of us. Let's just… agree to talk things through, when it gets tough. No matter what, we want what's best for the baby. That's all that matters.'

'Yes,' he said quietly, his voice low and raspy, and suddenly, Libby wasn't aware of their conversation or what had upset her, or even of the baby. Every fibre of her soul was focused on the man in front of her, standing so close that if she exhaled heavily, her breasts would brush his chest. She was aware of the feeling of his fingertips against her skin, his touch light, intended to be calming, but it was having the opposite effect on her frazzled nerves.

She blinked up at him and found herself in a time warp, the last few months evaporating in a deep well, sinking her back to the boat, that moment of connection, to how easy it had been when so overcome by the powerful emotions of survival to reach out and touch him, to feel and connect on a totally immersive level.

Raul's eyes were hooded, hard to read, but they dropped to her lips and stayed there, so Libby's pulse grew fast and erratic and she wondered if he could feel it somehow through her skin, if he could sense her response to him. Was he feeling it too?

She lifted her hand to his wrist, wrapped it around, fingers brushing his pulse point, but her own was too chaotic to make sense of his.

'Libby,' he murmured, frowning, his gaze moving to hers, probing her eyes as if he could read answers there, as if he could understand something important in the depths of her pupils.

'We shouldn't do this,' she said, even as she swayed forward, her body brushing his, and she felt the hiss of air escaping his lips, felt his chest jolt as he sucked in, and then his other hand was at her back, holding her right where she was, pressed to him, no more than a hair's breadth between their bodies. This was stupid and complicated, but it was also simple and right. What a strange and contradictory way to describe their situation, she thought as she lifted up onto the tips of her toes, her eyes holding his without fear.

His hand at her back moved higher, then lower, stroking her through the soft wool of her jumper, sending thousands of shockwaves through Libby, making her whole body reverberate with pleasure and awareness. Then he kissed her, slowly, gently, just the lightest brushing of his lips to hers at first, but that didn't matter.

The smallest spark can still ignite a forest, and the lightest touch of Raul's lips to Libby's was enough to remind them both of the heat that had burned between them that afternoon.

Raul groaned low in his throat and then… There was nothing light about his kiss, it was white-hot with a frantic need that turned her bones to mush and made her body tingle all over. Thought was no longer possible; she was simply a physical being, existing purely for this, for Raul.

Her hands pushed at his shirt, lifting it from the waistband of his trousers, fumbling with the buttons, yet persisting until they were undone and she could push it from his body, and then her fingertips roamed his flesh with impunity, touching him as she'd been desperate to do, she acknowledged only to herself, since that afternoon, when her dreams had been filled with memories she thought she'd never have the chance to relive.

He groaned again as her touch ran over his chest and to his shoulders, then her hands wrapped around his neck so her breasts were pressed to his torso and even through the fabric she wore her nipples grew taut and sensitive, tingling almost painfully.

He said her name like a curse but didn't break the kiss. Instead, he reached down and lifted Libby, wrapping her legs around his waist, carrying her easily through the penthouse, down the corridor and turning right, not left, taking her to his room rather than hers.

Inside, it was similar to Libby's, only bigger, with a more masculine décor—a huge bed sat in the centre, and at the sight of it, Libby's pulse went totally haywire, but there was no time to question this. Not when Raul was kissing her as though his life depended on it, not when he placed her on the ground and began to remove her clothes, not when his hands were worshipping her body, running over her, touching her, teasing her, tempting her, making it impossible to imagine a world in which they didn't come together.

'You are so beautiful,' he grunted, shaking his head with the appearance of disbelief as he removed the rest of his own clothes, rendering them both naked in the privacy of his bedroom. She wasn't nervous. It was as if she'd been preparing for this her whole life, as if there was nothing more vital or important.

'So are you,' she said honestly, artlessly, reaching out a hand, wanting to touch him again. He stepped forward, his Adam's apple jolting visibly as he swallowed. Libby touched the centre of his chest first and felt his breath draw inwards, then ran her fingers lower, down towards a dark arrow of hair that drew her to his manhood. Trembling a little, she let her fingers brush him, felt him jerk, and a rush of power made her smile.

'This is madness,' he said, eyes glittering when they met hers.

'I know. We really shouldn't.'

He nodded, standing still.

'Not after this.' She tilted her head, challenging him. 'Not again.'

He laughed softly, relief obvious in his features. 'You have yourself a deal,' he said with a nod, and then he was lifting her, carrying her to the bed, laying her down and kissing Libby with all the passion and promise she remembered, with everything she'd been craving and needing, and suddenly it didn't matter that their marriage was only a shadow of what she wanted. When he could make her feel like this, when there was pleasure as rich and as absorbing as Raul created, Libby cared for nothing else. This would be enough: it would have to be.

CHAPTER EIGHT

'CAN YOU MEET me in an hour?'

Libby's gaze shifted to the clock on the oven. 'Meet you where?'

He named a world-famous jeweller with a store on Fifth Avenue.

'Oh.' Libby's pulse trembled, not just because of the mention of a jeweller, but because the sound of Raul's voice alone had been enough to have that effect on her ever since they'd slept together the day before. They'd agreed it would be a one-off, so she wasn't stupid enough to be thinking about a repeat performance. At least, not consciously. But if she'd thought having sex with Raul would cure her of her cravings, she'd been wrong. If anything, it only stoked them further.

'Libby?'

She'd let her mind wander, and forced herself to focus now.

'I guess. But why?'

'You'll see.' He disconnected the call, leaving Libby frowning, holding the cell phone to her ear, staring out over a wintry Manhattan afternoon.

It was dark when her cab pulled up at the address she'd been given, the early sunsets par for the course at this time of year, and a hint of snow had started to fall, so Libby allowed herself a moment to stand and hold up her hands, catching some flakes in her gloves, smiling as she brought it near enough to her face to see the tiny little crystals.

'Beautiful,' she murmured to no one in particular, caught in the midst of a bustling group of people making their way down the street with little regard for the Australian who was enjoying her first real winter. Libby was so captivated by the glorious sight that she didn't notice Raul, standing by the door to the shop, his eyes having landed on her the moment she exited the taxi with unconscious grace.

Libby smiled to herself then dusted off her hands, preparing to move inside the shop, until a movement alerted her to Raul's presence. Her heart slammed into her ribs. She forced a smile but she was self-conscious suddenly, embarrassed by her childlike love for the phenomenon of snow.

'I'm not used to it,' she explained with a lift of her shoulders as she approached him.

His eyes skimmed her features. 'I remember my first winter here. It was a shock to the system.'

'But so wonderful,' Libby said on a happy sigh. 'I think it's gloriously beautiful.'

He lifted a brow and then surprised them both by laughing. 'Has anyone ever told you you're the most optimistic person they've ever met?'

Heat burned in Libby's cheeks. 'No, actually.'

'Well, I'm sure they've thought it. Are you ready?'

'What for, exactly?'

He put a hand at Libby's lower back, shepherding her through the large revolving door. 'To choose your ring.'

Libby stopped walking in the middle of the spinning door, only to receive a bump on the bottom as the glass kept rotating.

'Oh. Can't you just pick something? Something simple,' she added.

'I don't know you well enough to know what you'd like,' he pointed out. 'And as you'll be wearing it every day for a long time, it should be something you don't hate, right?'

Every day for a long time. Not, she noticed, *for ever.* Because once their child was old enough, they'd be able to dispense with this ruse and go their separate ways, and she was sure they were both looking forward to that.

Libby forced a tight smile. 'Okay. Let's just have a casual look around.'

Only Raul didn't do anything casually, and the name Raul Ortega clearly opened the kinds of doors Libby had never even known existed. Far from being allowed to 'look around', they were greeted by a personal concierge, who insisted on taking them to a private room to view rings in comfort. Not only were they placed side by side on a small sofa so their thighs brushed the whole time, they were brought a trolley stacked with food and drinks then left completely alone whilst the staff assembled several boxes of beautiful rings.

Libby found the silence stretched her nerves almost to breaking point. It was the closest they'd been since making love and her heart was ramming against her chest in a way she wasn't sure was entirely safe. But the more she thought about Raul, about the things he'd said yesterday, his childhood, and reflected on the way he'd been when he saw the sonogram, the more she knew he was quicksand. He was the definition of emotionally distant, and the last thing she should do was let herself get swept up in the crazy, red-hot passion that sparked between them.

'About yesterday,' Libby finally said, figuring it was better to address the elephant in the room.

Beside her, Raul stiffened. 'I know. It shouldn't have happened.' He turned to face her, and Libby's stomach was suddenly hollow. 'We'll be more careful from now on.'

It was exactly what Libby had been going to say, but hearing it from Raul did something strange to her insides, and made her breathing strain. Before she could figure out how to respond, a woman walked in with two display cases of rings, and from then on it was impossible to talk about anything except the clarity of diamonds.

Raul had always run.

As a boy he'd loved the freedom, the feeling of wind in his hair, the strength in his legs, the burning in his lungs. He'd been carted from foster home to foster home, each situation offering new challenges and dangers, but always he'd had his own strength and speed. He'd slipped out of bed early most mornings, before anyone else woke, and he would run as far and fast as he could. It hadn't mattered to him that the streets weren't always safe; that had added to the thrill. Danger couldn't catch him; he'd outrun it.

When he'd left the foster system for good and wound up living rough, he'd run even when his belly had been so empty the exercise had cost him vital energy. He'd run because it was an inherent part of him—to know he could take himself wherever he needed to go, whenever necessary.

Running was a habit for Raul, and it was also where he did his best thinking, taking whatever problem he faced at that point in time and untangling the knots until it made sense to him. Usually, he focused on business, his mind effortlessly trawling over his current circumstances, reorganising the pieces, shuffling, until he happened upon a solution.

This morning, as the sun was just starting to hint its golden promise over the city, he found his mind singularly turned to Libby. Only each step he took brought him closer to confusion, not clarity, so he ran harder, faster, waiting for something to loosen in his mind, to offer comprehension, an understanding of their situation.

He was attracted to her.

And she was attracted to him.

So what?

He'd been attracted to women before. He'd slept with women. This wasn't new, for either of them. The only difference was that his baby was growing inside of her and, despite the fact he'd sworn he'd never have a family, he couldn't help but feel a biological connection to that child and, by extension, to Libby.

That was why this felt different, he realised as he hit the six-mile mark. It wasn't about them *per se*, but the fact they were going to be co-parenting. It was an intimate relationship regardless of the reality of their situation: that they barely knew one another.

Sleeping together didn't mean anything. It was an itch they'd scratched. And despite what they'd said, he suspected they'd scratch it again when they wanted to.

That didn't have to be complicated. It didn't have to change anything.

And yet surely it was smarter to keep things in their own clear lane.

They were getting married for the sake of this baby. They were going to be living together, raising a child together. Just the thought of that made Raul's throat constrict with panic. So much so, he had to stop running a moment, pressing his hands to his hips and sucking in big bursts of cold morning air.

He didn't want this, he thought with a groan. He didn't want to be tied to anyone.

He was a runner. He ran. He ran whenever he wanted or needed to. He didn't have belongings he cared enough about to lose. He didn't have people he cared enough about to lose. He couldn't care about a child or a wife. He couldn't.

And yet, what choice did he have? He was about to become a father—it was a sacred role, one he knew he would fulfil because he'd experienced only absence there. In his heart, where he might have turned to find love and strength built from generations of support, he knew nothing. It was a void he would never pass on to his child. He had to be in their life; this was the only option.

He was terrified of the steps he was taking, terrified of a future tethered to anyone, and somehow Libby made that all the more frightening, yet he knew he had to act fast, to make this happen.

For even though he was afraid and acknowledged this to be the last thing he wanted, at the same time he also understood he wouldn't breathe easily until Libby was officially his wife and their commitment to this child was formalised.

And there it was. The clarity he'd sought.

Many times in Raul's life he'd been afraid and yet he'd acted. If anything, the fear made him more determined: he wouldn't be cowed by it. He'd been afraid to turn up at each new foster home, afraid of the new rules, the new people, the new environments, the new schools. Afraid and yet determined never to show it: he conquered fear and doubt with strength and courage, and he would do so again.

Running once more, he began to formulate a plan, meeting the uncertainty of his heart with black and white steps of determination and action.

That, after all, was Raul's way.

Libby read the email with a strange heaving in her chest.

Libby
The wedding will take place on Friday at two p.m., after which we'll have a late lunch to celebrate.
R

She read it again, frowning now, her heart pounding against her ribs.

The wedding will take place on Friday at two p.m.

There was no mention of how she'd get to the wedding, no mention of a honeymoon, no mention of any of the specifics that she wanted to know. But what he had mentioned was enough to send her pulse into total disarray.

Friday was only two days away.

Two days!

She knew they were getting married quickly, but foolishly hadn't expected it would happen so soon. And yet, wasn't that the whole point of this? He'd taken her to buy a wedding ring; that had clearly been a forerunner to the event itself.

...after which we'll have a late lunch to celebrate.

Celebrate what? Their sham wedding?

Her lips pulled to the side as she felt a familiar emptiness in her heart, the pain of knowing how far removed their wedding and marriage were from what she'd always wanted. But she forced herself to ignore it. This wasn't about her. She'd already grappled with the sacrifice she was making, and why.

For their baby, she'd do this. She'd make it work. And she refused to feel sad about it—there was just no point in lamenting what she could never have. She'd have to find a different kind of fairy tale, and she suspected that would begin and end with the love she felt for the little person growing inside her belly.

He arrived late that night, and Libby was already asleep; Raul left early the next morning, and so on and so forth, so on the morning of their wedding she awoke with a strange sense of absence warring with anticipation in the pit of her stomach.

She was getting married today, to a man she hadn't seen nor spoken to in days, and despite the pragmatic circumstances behind their union, her stomach was filled with butterflies and she couldn't help the hum in her bloodstream as she dressed with care for the ceremony.

It was not in a church.

She wouldn't carry a long, trailing bouquet like Queen Elizabeth's—the flowers she'd always fantasised about—but that didn't matter. She was focusing beyond the wedding, on the marriage, and the baby. Once this formality was dealt with, she could start giving her attention to setting up Raul's apartment for the arrival of their child.

It would feel real then.

Important to start preparing, decorating a nursery, buying clothes, getting ready for the reality of parenthood. There'd be childbirth classes too, and playgroups she could join.

Libby found great solace in turning her mind to those practical, baby-led plans, and she thought purely of their child as she dressed for the wedding.

She'd chosen a simple outfit, befitting the simple ceremony they'd be having, and at one o'clock she was preparing to go downstairs and hail a cab when the lift to the penthouse opened and Raul strode in, wearing a jet-black tuxedo with a snow-white shirt.

He was the last person Libby expected to see: in fact, she'd thought she wouldn't see him for another hour, and not here but at the office where their wedding was to take place, and so her jaw dropped and her eyes widened.

'You're not supposed to be here,' she blurted out. 'It's bad luck.'

His look was one of pure cynicism. 'I think that horse has bolted, don't you?'

She didn't need reminding, on their wedding day, of all days, that he found the whole situation unlucky. Libby's response was a tight smile. 'I presumed we'd be meeting there.'

'I brought you these.'

It was then that Libby noticed he was carrying a crisp white bag. She frowned, walking towards him, and when he extended it, she saw a bouquet of white roses inside, with baby's breath poked in between. The bouquet was held together with a cream ribbon made of wide satin and pinned down the seam with pearls.

'Oh,' she said, staring at it, her mouth dry. It wasn't what she had imagined and yet somehow it was lovely, and all the more so because he'd thought to arrange it for her. 'Thank you.'

He nodded. 'The photographer will meet us there.'

'Photographer?' she repeated, the detail yet another she'd presumed would be absent.

'For wedding photos.'

She rolled her eyes. 'I know what photographers do. I just didn't think we'd have one.'

'It's the done thing, isn't it?'

'Maybe for real weddings, but do either of us really want to remember this day?'

His eyes narrowed imperceptibly and a muscle jerked in his jaw. 'It's not for us. Our son or daughter will appreciate seeing a photo in the future, I'm sure.'

'Right,' she agreed. This ruse was all for the baby. 'Good thinking.'

'Do you need to eat anything before we go?'

She shook her head. 'I couldn't possibly.' Libby bit down on her lip. 'I'm filled with butterflies.'

He lifted a brow.

'Nerves,' she clarified.

'Why would you be nervous?'

'Because I'm getting married, and to someone I don't know particularly well,' she pointed out. 'It's weird and strange and even though I know this isn't a real marriage, I still feel like I'm about to do something momentous and important.' She shrugged. 'Aren't you?'

'Nervous?'

She nodded once.

'No.'

'Really? Not even a little?'

His eyes skimmed her face. 'You'll feel better when it's over.'

She grimaced. 'Like having a tooth pulled?'

His lips flicked in an unexpected smile. 'Exactly.'

'But no lidocaine.'

'It'll be mostly harmless. Over within minutes.'

She nodded, wishing the knots in her tummy would straighten out. Wishing that he understood the lack of fanfare was all part of the broader problem. She pressed a hand to her belly, not to feel the little life there but in the hope of straightening out her anxiety, and instead felt worse.

'Okay,' she said a little unevenly. 'Let's do this.'

The whole thing was surreal. She felt as though she were living in a sort of dream as they descended in the lift to the street level, where a limousine was waiting. They rode side by side and in silence to the hall. Confetti and rose petals were strewn on the steps, remnants of other marriages, presumably happier, more genuine matches.

Libby ignored the sight of it, ignored the pulling in her belly, ignored, most of all, the feeling that this was all so very, very wrong. It was for the baby, she kept reminding herself as she walked up the steps at Raul's side, into the beautiful old building with marble floors and wood panelling.

A simple sign pointed towards the *Register Office for Civil Unions.*

'I guess that's us,' she said, blinking up at Raul, wondering if she was waiting for him to change his mind, to say this wasn't their best idea, that they could wait.

But he didn't. He nodded once, his lips a grim line in his face, and she knew he was feeling as ambivalent about this as she was, even though he wouldn't admit it.

He put a hand against the base of her spine and, despite her anxiety, Libby trembled, her body surging in response and awareness, which she bitterly resented. How could she feel such contradictory emotions?

The hall was long and brightly lit, by windows on one side and electric bulbs overhead. Libby walked beside Raul, one foot in front of the other, until they reached a wooden door. Their names were on a printed piece of paper stuck to a noticeboard out front.

Two p.m. Ortega & Langham.

Libby's pulse was thready. She sucked in a deep breath, found it impossible to look at Raul, so stared at the wood grain of the door until she had practically memorised the pattern. Finally, a moment after two p.m., the doors opened and a young couple stepped out, a woman with bright red hair and a man wearing a kilt. They were too busy embracing, laughing, to notice Raul and Libby, and she was glad. She didn't want anyone to see her in that moment, the pallor of her skin, the slight trembling of her body—she was sure she must look like the most unexcited bride there'd ever been.

Only, even in that state of mind, Libby found herself trying to focus on the positives. To ignore her nerves and see the beauty of the room they were shepherded into, and the gift she was giving her child by marrying Raul. She wasn't old-fashioned enough to believe this was the only way to raise a little person; of course she didn't. But for Libby, having grown up with such insecurity in her life, she knew that for *her* it was the right choice. She wanted to give this child the world, and Raul could make that happen. Not just because he was wealthy beyond belief, but because in this one vital area they were in complete agreement. Nothing mattered more than their baby's future, their baby's security, their baby's happiness.

The ceremony was swift. Raul and Libby took turns repeating their vows, then exchanged rings. Libby was surprised Raul had one for himself. She hadn't even thought he would want to wear a ring, and yet when the time came he produced a simple band from his pocket, placed it in her palm, then waited, hand outstretched, for her to slide it onto his finger. Her own fingers trembled as she did so, and it took her a few turns, but Raul waited with no expression on his face as she performed the act, binding them, in the eyes of the law, 'till death do us part'.

It was an indication of Libby's mindset that she hadn't even thought of the conclusion of the ceremony until the moment was upon them. As the celebrant said, 'Congratulations, you may now kiss the bride,' Libby's heart jolted and she turned to Raul, wide-eyed, blinking up at him with consternation.

She wasn't prepared for this.

She felt too vulnerable, as though she didn't have her armour in place; she felt that she needed time to adjust to being married before having to kiss him, and yet it was a formality, part and parcel of the ruse they'd just completed. She stood there, too aware of every breath in her body, every throb of her heart, every pulse of her blood, every organ, every thought, every memory; it was all there, evoked inside Libby, swirling like a tornado, obliterating consciousness and time.

Raul moved slowly, his hand coming around her back, drawing her to him, as if giving her time to demur, to tell him to stop.

She didn't. She was very still, totally passive, waiting, heart on edge.

His other hand came to her face, tilted her chin towards him, and then his head bent slowly, cautiously, his eyes closing so his lashes formed two thick, dark fans against his cheeks right before his mouth claimed hers and she moaned softly as a rush of feelings overcame her.

Anxiety was gone. Nervousness and uncertainty disappeared.

Every little piece of her that had been shaky and on edge locked hard into place, so she was Libby again, but not as she'd ever been before. She was like a butterfly emerging from a chrysalis, no longer Libby Langham but Libby Ortega—different, beautiful, strong, married and a mother-to-be. These thoughts were blades cutting through the back of her mind without her awareness. All Libby could feel was the rightness of this kiss, the warmth of his hand on her back, the pleasure of his touch at her cheek, the flicking of his tongue against hers, a delicious, tempting, sinful dance that was laced with promise and anticipation.

She was lost, utterly, and she knew she should fight that, that she should do whatever she could to hold onto herself in all this madness, but being lost to Raul was one of the best things she'd ever felt, and on her wedding day, of all days, shouldn't Libby allow herself that one little indulgence?

CHAPTER NINE

RAUL PULLED AWAY for a moment, staring down at Libby as though he'd never seen her before, as though he'd never seen a flesh and blood woman in his life, his eyes sweeping across her face, trying to make sense of it, but even then there was a magnetic pull towards her that dominated all else, and suddenly he was kissing her again, his mouth on hers more demanding, more urgent, reminding him of the first cataclysmic time they'd touched. He'd put it down to adrenalin then, and maybe the same excuse applied now—their wedding day was not a moment without emotion for either of them, despite the nature of their union. Whatever the reason, he wanted to kiss her. He didn't question that want, he simply drew her into his arms and took what she was offering, with no thought of where they were nor how out of step this was with their marriage.

It didn't *feel* out of step.

It felt like exactly what he should be doing, and she tasted so sweet, like vanilla and strawberries, so he wanted more and more of her. Her dress was a simple silk with a white faux fur coat. She was a sensory explosion, all soft and textural beneath his touch.

He suddenly wanted to be anywhere but here, in a

room in a courthouse, being married by some strange officiant. As if on cue, the man cleared his throat, perhaps more than once, but it took a moment for Raul to hear, to recollect himself and pull away from Libby, to stare down at her with an expression more like the impassive mask he should have been wearing.

'Thank you,' he said, not sure if he was speaking to Libby or the celebrant, but extending a hand in the celebrant's direction belatedly.

'Congratulations.' The man grinned, gesturing to the door. 'If you'll head out there, Rowena will see to the paperwork.'

In his peripheral vision, Raul saw Libby's tight nod of her head, and a single glance in her direction showed the dazed and confused look on her face. Something tightened inside of him. He had to get control of this. He had to manage things better.

As they signed the certificate of marriage, the photographer Raul's assistant had organised took pictures and Raul made a point of smiling, remembering the whole purpose of this was to have something to show their child when they were older. Perhaps they'd even print one of the pictures and hang it on a wall. Raul didn't have any photographs of himself or his birth parents, or anyone of significance in his life. There'd never really been anyone, and that was fine by Raul, but for their child they were creating a different reality, a myth, and pictures would be a part of that.

In front of the building, they posed for a few more snaps, but when the photographer suggested a kiss Raul responded gruffly, 'That's enough.' He felt Libby stiffen at his side and could have kicked himself. 'It's cold. Time

to get inside,' he said, turning to Libby and offering another smile—though it felt stretched on his face.

She nodded, not meeting his eyes.

Back in the limousine, he noticed they sat as far from
one another as possible. Good. Keeping their distance
was a wise move.

'You mentioned something about a lunch now?' she
asked quietly, fidgeting with her hands in her lap.

Raul closed his eyes as he remembered that particular
detail. 'My assistant's idea.'

He missed the hurt on Libby's face, but when she
spoke her voice trembled a little. 'We don't have to go.
There's not really anything to celebrate here, is there?'

Raul cursed inwardly. 'We just got married,' he said.
'It's the least we can do to mark the occasion.'

'I really can't see that's necessary,' she muttered, the
glumness in her voice unmistakable, and she continued
to stare at her wedding ring.

Raul reached over, putting a hand on hers without
thinking, then wishing he hadn't when he felt the now
predictable surge of awareness travel the length of his
arm. Touching her was his weakness. The lightest brush
of his flesh to hers and he forgot everything he'd promised himself about this marriage, the necessary boundaries and restrictions, and just wanted to exist without
constraint.

'We are having a child, and raising them as a family.
We both know why that matters to us.'

'Yes,' she whispered, lifting her head but only so she
could tilt it away from him, looking out of the window.

'So let's celebrate our commitment to the baby,' he
said. 'This is the first day of our new family,' he said,

and Libby turned to face him then, eyes wide and so beautiful he couldn't look away.

'Family,' she murmured, as if struck by that idea. Just as he was when he heard her say the word. Struck, and trapped. Terrified. He removed his hand, tried not to look as though the heavens were falling down around him.

'Besides, I'm hungry.'

Libby nodded, then blinked and turned away. Raul resisted the urge to ask her to turn back, to look at him again, but her eyes were quickly becoming an addiction of his. Yet another thing to conquer.

Not only was the restaurant beautiful and exclusive, but Raul's assistant had outdone herself, having a small private alcove reserved for the occasion, decked out in dozens more of the stunning white roses that had formed Libby's bouquet. She brushed the petals of one as she sat down, the softness reminding her of the silk of her dress.

'You look beautiful,' Raul said, as if reading her mind, like he was also thinking of the silk she wore.

Heat suffused Libby's cheeks. 'It's just a thrift shop find,' she said. 'A bit of fun, really. The dress is from the twenties.'

'It suits you.'

'I guess I'm an old-fashioned kind of girl,' she quipped, eyes dropping to her wedding ring, a frown tugging at her lips before she could control it.

A waitress appeared with a bottle of champagne, popped the top. 'It's non-alcoholic,' she said with a bright smile, 'per the request we were emailed.'

They were silent as the drinks were poured, and then, left to their own devices, that silence took on a crackling, electric quality. Libby reached for her drink, wrapped her fingers around the stem but didn't lift it.

'A toast,' Raul said quietly. Libby waited, heart in her throat. 'To our baby's future,' he murmured, and it was so perfectly appropriate because it was a heartfelt sentiment, perhaps the only heartfelt utterance he could have delivered in that moment, and it meant the world to both of them. Libby lifted her glass and clinked it to his.

'To our baby,' she murmured, sipping the drink, finding it every bit as delicious as champagne. She closed her eyes, the moment wrapping around her. 'I can't believe we're married,' she said after a beat.

'I was there. It happened.'

She pulled a face. 'Yeah, I just mean…'

'I know what you mean.'

'In the blink of an eye, I feel like my life has changed so much.' She looked around the room, gesturing distractedly to the grandeur of the restaurant. 'I mean, look at this place. It's the sort of restaurant my clients go to, not me.'

Raul was a study in relaxation. 'What did you see as your future, Libby?'

'I hadn't worked it out yet,' she said honestly. 'I thought I'd study, do something so I could work from home and take care of the baby.'

He nodded. 'I mean if there was no baby. Before meeting me, what was your long-term plan? At one time you wanted to be a chef. But after that, was there anything else?'

It wasn't an unreasonable question and yet, for some reason, Libby felt her defensive hackles rise. 'I didn't think about it. I just had to work and earn enough to get by.'

'I admire that,' he surprised her by saying. 'But surely at some point you wanted something more?'

'No.' She ran a finger over the condensation on her glass. 'Although...'

'What?'

'It's stupid,' she said with a wry smile, but the smile slipped when she saw the look in his eyes—a look of such intense interest that heat bubbled in her veins. 'When I was a kid, I wanted to be a doctor.'

Raul lifted one brow. 'Why is that stupid?'

'Well, I can't stand the sight of blood, for one thing,' she said, sipping her drink. 'But when I was a little girl, maybe seven or eight, my mum passed out. She'd had too much to drink, but I didn't know that then. I just remember seeing her on the floor, not being able to wake her up and panicking. We'd had firefighters come to our school earlier that year, talking to us about what to do in an emergency, so I knew to call emergency services. An ambulance came with flashing lights and kind, confident people who made me feel so good and like everything was going to be okay. My mother was *furious* with me,' she added, grimacing.

'Why?'

'For one thing, she was embarrassed. For another, there was a cost for the callout.' Libby scrunched up her nose. 'But I'll never forget my sense of helplessness, contrasted with the relief I felt when the paramedics arrived and knew exactly what to do. I wanted to be that person who could walk into a room and fix people, make everything okay for everyone.' Libby bit down on her lip. 'Instead, I clean houses. And boats.'

Raul reached across the table, put his hand on Libby's, and her heart jumped into her throat. She felt his sympathy and immediately wanted to push it away.

'It's not like I hate it,' she said. 'In fact, there's a lot to like about it. The pay's okay, and I get to choose my schedule.'

'Not to mention the occasional adventure on the high seas,' he pointed out.

'Right.' She was surprised by how natural it felt to smile. The waitress returned to take their orders. Libby hadn't even looked at the options. Raul suggested a tasting menu and she readily agreed.

'You have some food allergies though, right?' the waitress said, referring to her notepad.

Raul spoke before Libby could respond. 'Shellfish and soft cheeses.'

Libby's eyes widened. He'd read the pregnancy books? Of course he had. Raul was taking no chances with this baby. Her stomach did a funny little loop.

'Got it.' The waitress smiled as she departed.

Libby propped her elbows on the table, resting her chin on one palm. 'What about you?' she asked, fascinated by the strength in Raul's face, the symmetry of his features. 'What did you want to be when you were a kid?'

He grinned. 'A builder.'

'Really?'

'I loved watching high-rises go up. I was fascinated by the way they could be shaped almost as if from the ground. The steel, concrete, the structures. I would skip school and watch the work all day. Sometimes, I'd get to help, earn a few bucks. I loved the feeling of creating something with my bare hands,' he said, looking down at them, almost as if surprised by the admission. 'I haven't thought of that for a long time.'

'But instead you became…well, fabulously wealthy,' she said, crinkling her nose again. 'I don't even know what you do, besides make a lot of money.'

'I started off investing in companies,' he said, as though it were that simple.

'What kinds of companies?'

'Businesses that were failing but which had untapped potential. I exploited their market weakness to get a good deal, then either restructured to turn a profit or pieced them up and sold them off, whichever was going to yield the best return.'

She shook her head. 'I can't even imagine how you got started doing that,' she murmured. 'As someone who comes from nothing, who never had money behind me, just getting by is a struggle some days.'

'Yes,' he agreed with vehemence. 'Precisely. I hit rock-bottom, Libby. I hit it, scraped along it, settled there for long enough to know that I couldn't keep living like that. I had to claw my way off the bottom with my bare hands. It was bloody and hard, and I had to fight tooth and nail to get out, but I swore to myself I would never know that kind of poverty again. I would never be hungry, I would never be cold, I would never be on the streets.'

Admiration for Raul's determination swelled inside of her, and a pride too that she immediately fought. After all, what business did she have feeling proud of him? None of this was down to her. He wasn't even her real husband. It was a sobering thought and her smile momentarily slipped.

'I got a job at a construction company. Just a small one, run by an old couple—they were in their late eighties when I met them. I don't know why they hired me. I was as surprised then as I am now. I was seventeen, skinnier than a nail, but they took a bet on me and I wasn't going to waste the opportunity. I worked my fingers to the bone, and the owner's wife, Maria, would bring lunches to the site. She must have seen how hungry I was. I ate, gained weight, grew stronger, worked harder. I worked for them for three years, got to know them, and then the owner, Pedro, came to me one day and told me he was retiring. That he was leaving the company to me. It was a gift, Libby. A gift. Only, he didn't see it that way. He said I would take their legacy and turn it into something great. He said that he believed in me.'

Raul's eyes widened and Libby's heart felt dangerously soft and aching. 'No one had *ever* believed in me before. It was a gift and a burden. I have spent the last ten years trying to justify his faith.'

Libby's eyes were suspiciously moist. 'Do you still own the company?'

'It's the backbone of all that I do,' Raul admitted. 'It's basically unrecognisable now, but I kept the name, and I think of Maria and Pedro often, I wonder where I would have been if it weren't for them.'

'They didn't have children?'

'No. They couldn't.'

Libby grimaced sympathetically. 'They must have felt that they won the lottery, finding you.'

'I try to make decisions they would be proud of,' he

said, again looking surprised by the admission. 'I try to justify the gift they gave me.'

'Raul, even without them, I have no doubt you would be sitting here right now. There's just something about you. Pedro and Maria saw it; I do too.'

His eyes flicked to hers then away again, almost as if he didn't want to believe that.

'Do you ever think about those guys who stole your boat?' she asked, sipping her drink, then easing back in her seat as the waitress appeared with their entrees, a delightful little bowl of velouté.

'Think about them in what way?'

'Wonder about their lives, what they're doing now?'

'I know what they're doing,' he answered simply.

She blinked. She supposed it was possible the police had kept Raul in the loop, given they'd tried to steal his boat.

'Two have been moved into apprenticeship programmes to learn a trade, one is at a boarding school in the city, and another is being helped by a social worker with some childhood trauma he experienced.'

Libby paused, midway through lifting her spoon from the bowl. 'How do you know this?'

Raul briefly looked uncomfortable.

Libby's heart sped up. 'You did that for them, didn't you?'

'Punishment of a judicial nature didn't seem to fit the crime. Besides, I know what kids like that need, and it's not detention.'

Her stomach was in knots and tears sprang to her eyes quickly.

Raul looked terrified.

'I'm sorry.' Libby half laughed. 'It's the pregnancy hormones.' But it wasn't, and she shook her head, dispelling that. 'No, it's more, it's… I think you did a wonderful thing for them,' she said softly. 'Maria and Pedro would be so proud of you.'

Raul looked away before she could see his response, but she knew she'd touched a chord deep within him.

'It was the right thing to do.'

'Yeah,' she agreed in a heartbeat. 'But lots of people wouldn't have done it. I mean, they punched you—'

'He caught me off-guard. He was little more than a child.'

'Still. They stole your boat.'

'I got it back. No harm done. Besides, a boat is just a boat. It's a thing, easy to replace.'

She shook her head. 'Not necessarily, but for you, yes, I can see your point.'

They ate their soup and Libby was surprised to find they slipped easily into small talk. She asked him about the city and he returned those questions, so she found herself sharing stories of her walking adventures, how far she'd gone, how much of the city she'd seen by exploring on foot. He asked about her favourite streets, any cafés she'd found and enjoyed, if there was anything she'd wanted to do but couldn't, and Libby realised she had been developing a wish-list as she'd walked, of certain sights she'd like to tour, shops she wanted to explore.

'It's just all so different to what I'm used to,' she said. 'The weather, the streets, the buildings.' She shook her head. 'I realise how sheltered I've been, in not travelling. You know, I'd only ever flown once before meeting you,' she confided. 'To Brisbane, for Mum's funeral.'

Raul's expression was unchanged but something shifted in the depth of his gaze.

'Now I feel as though my eyes have been opened to this whole big wide world and I want to see it, Raul. I want to explore everything.'

'Where else would you like to go?' he asked, as the waitress came to clear their plates. Libby didn't notice.

'Oh, I don't mean I want to leave New York,' she said with a wave of her hand. 'Only that I want to inhale this city while I'm here. I want to see and understand everything. And yes, then I'd like to see more, cities I've read about and seen in movies and never thought I would have within my reach. I want to show them to our child, to explore them together,' she said, smiling as she patted her stomach.

'And you will. You know my plane is at your disposal, I presume?'

Libby's eyes went round in her face. 'Erm...no, I didn't, actually, but I...' Her voice trailed off as she realised how foolish she'd been about to sound. To actually admit that part of what she'd been envisaging was exploring not just with their child but with Raul too.

She coloured to the roots of her hair. 'Thank you, I'll keep that in mind.'

CHAPTER TEN

HE'D SAID SOMETHING WRONG, though he had no idea what it could possibly have been. He was doing everything he could to make this easier for Libby, to offer her what he thought she wanted.

Here she was, sitting across from him, painting him a picture of a life without wings, a life in which she'd been trapped in a rut of hard work and little pleasure, from what he could tell, aside from her God-given ability to derive happiness from the mundane. So he was offering her the keys to the world and he wanted her to use them. He wanted her to realise that their marriage, while necessary for this baby, was not a prison sentence so much as a chance for freedom for her.

Because it was important to assuage his guilt at having pressured her into this?

He could have supported her financially, he could have made her dreams come true without marrying her, but he'd manipulated her emotions, preying on the similarities in their backgrounds to push her into this.

For the sake of their baby, he reminded himself, shifting a little uneasily in his chair, frustrated that the relaxed atmosphere had evaporated and the air was once more crackling with tension and, damn it, awareness.

He didn't want to be aware of his wife.

He didn't want to be aware of the way her silky hair brushed her soft cheeks, of the way her lips parted when she expelled those little sighs, of the way her dress clung to her body like a second skin, of her slender hands as she reached for her champagne flute and took another delicate sip of non-alcoholic wine.

He didn't want to be aware of her in a way that made it dangerously simple to recall the way she'd felt as he'd sunk into her, making her his in a way that had sung to his soul.

'You work very long hours,' she said stiltedly into the silence of the room, and he barely heard her at first because he was absorbed by his own self-critical thoughts.

'Yes,' he agreed eventually.

Libby frowned. 'Is that…have you always?'

'Yes.'

'So it's not just since we…since I got here?'

His brows drew together. 'Do you mean, am I avoiding you?'

'It had crossed my mind,' she said with a lift of one brow.

'My job is demanding.' That wasn't strictly true, though. It didn't have to be. Raul micromanaged out of habit but, for the most part, his team of executives was more than capable of running things with significantly less involvement from Raul. 'It's hard for me to let go,' he explained after a beat. 'I am, I suppose, what you might call a control freak.'

'I'm shocked to hear that,' she said deadpan, and he laughed.

'I probably make my executives' lives hell,' he muttered. 'But it's something about having known that poverty, having been given the gift of a second chance from Maria and Pedro… I can't squander it.'

'So you're afraid that if you take your foot off the accelerator you might lose everything?'

'I'm not afraid of that,' he said thoughtfully. 'And I don't need anywhere near what I have. The money is beside the point. I'm not really that motivated by wealth. Once you can afford to have a roof over your head and three square meals a day, the rest is cream.'

'So what are you motivated by, then?'

'I like to win,' he said simply. 'Succeeding in business is a good metric of victory, don't you think?'

Her smile was enigmatic, as though she were thinking things she wouldn't say. 'I suppose so.'

But that bothered him and he couldn't understand why. 'You don't agree?'

'Success in life is better.'

'How do you measure success in life?'

Libby hesitated, looking self-conscious.

'You can say it,' he murmured, wondering why he was so desperate to hear whatever confession she'd been about to offer.

'I gave this a lot of thought, growing up.' She cleared her throat, then paused as the waitress returned with another course, setting the plates onto the table before disappearing. Libby's eyes fell to the food, but she looked distracted. 'I never wanted much. Just something different to my own experience of home life. For me—' she lifted her gaze then, piercing Raul with the intensity and purity in her eyes '—it was simple. I just wanted a family.' Her voice hitched as she spoke and something rolled uncomfortably in his gut. 'My biggest aspiration was being in a happy marriage, with an army of kids,' she added, a tight smile doing nothing to take away from the sting of her words.

Because how could Raul fail to hear the accusation in them, even when Libby had said and done nothing to make him feel that way? Their marriage, by its very nature, was a death knell to the hopes and dreams she'd clung to since childhood. They would have just one child, not an army. Raul could barely comprehend becoming a father at all—the idea of parenting more than one child was anathema to him. As for their marriage, while they'd agreed it would be based on respect and a level of friendship, it was never going to be the rosy, heart-warming vision Libby craved.

'Sometimes life doesn't work out how you plan it,' he said gruffly. 'But that doesn't mean it cannot still be a good life.'

'I know,' she answered without missing a beat, expelling a quick sigh and fidgeting her fingers. 'It's okay. I always thought I would find someone who was like my other half. My soulmate. That I'd fall crazy, head over heels in love and live happily ever after,' she added on a small laugh. 'But that's a fairy tale. A silly, juvenile dream.' She rubbed her hand over her stomach. 'I love our baby, Raul. That's enough for me.'

He hoped with all his heart she was being honest, because it was the best he could offer.

Libby stared at the ceiling, ignoring the pang in the centre of her chest.

It wasn't how she'd imagined spending her wedding

night. Not that she'd spent much time imagining anything, but deep down, if she were honest, she'd hoped for more than this. She'd hoped against hope for love, real love, and no matter what she said to Raul, she'd never be able to ignore the emptiness inside her chest.

But she had to.

She had to learn.

Libby knew that Raul was right: life didn't always work out how you wanted. In fact, in Libby's experience, most of the time it didn't. Being happy was a question of choice, and she'd *always* chosen happiness. She'd found pleasure in the small things in her life—the golden splash of sunshine against a newly painted fence, the smell of spring in the air and freshly cut grass, the feeling of wet sand underfoot—the things that were hers to marvel at and appreciate without anyone having the power to remove those small delights.

And she knew that the key to her future happiness relied on her ability to keep doing exactly that. To focus on the relief of being liberated from financial stress, the pleasure of growing life inside her belly, of knowing that while Raul might not love her, at least he loved their baby enough to want to be in their life. He would be a great father to their child, and for that she knew she had to be grateful. It had to be enough.

A week after their wedding Raul read his assistant's email for the tenth time, a strange presentiment in his gut.

Will Mrs Ortega be joining you?

Such a simple, and normal, request. After all, Justine would naturally presume that, in the first flush of new-lywed bliss, the couple wouldn't want to be separated. Raul hadn't explained to anyone except his lawyers the real reason for their marriage. It was no one's business.

But what could he say in response?

Just a flat-out no? It wasn't Raul's practice to explain himself to anyone, so why start now?

However, given the necessity of a trip to Rome, the thought of leaving Libby at home made him feel like a bastard. He grimaced ruefully. It wasn't about explaining himself to Justine, it was the thought of telling Libby that he was going to Europe and not bringing her. He'd wanted her to feel that this marriage was her chance to grow wings, hadn't he?

Was this a way to assuage his conscience at what he knew he'd taken away from her? That being the hope of ever living out her childhood hopes and dreams for a fairy tale happy ending?

Yes, he thought, standing with frustration and pacing across his office. That was precisely the problem. He had a guilty conscience and he didn't want to feel worse than he already did.

She'd cover her response quickly, he was sure, but she'd still feel it. Hurt. Offended. As if he couldn't bear to be with her. Besides, it wasn't like they would need to spend time together if she were to come. Rome was a big city and Raul was travelling for work. So long as he spelled that out when he invited her it would be fine.

With a growl low in his throat that spoke of the regret

he knew he'd feel no matter what he chose, he moved back to his keyboard and typed out a reply before he could change his mind.

Yes.

'Libby?'

She glanced at the bedside clock, frowning. It was after ten, and she'd been about to slip into bed.

'Yes?'

'Have you got a moment?'

She glanced at her reflection in the mirror with a sense of panic. Her pyjamas were hardly the last word in seduction—she wore a pair of comfortable yoga pants and a singlet top but, nonetheless, the idea of Raul seeing her like this did something funny to her insides.

'Libby?' His voice was stern, and it put paid to her indecision.

'Okay.' She wrenched the door inwards and almost lost her footing because he was *right there*, all handsome and businesslike in a button-down shirt with the sleeves pushed up to his elbows, and dark grey trousers that emphasised his slim waist. Her mouth felt dry and her heart fluttered. But it was the way Raul looked at her that sent Libby's pulse into dangerously fast territory. His eyes rested on her face for the briefest moment before travelling all the way down her body, landing on her pale, bare feet, then moving up and clinging to her slightly rounded stomach, so she lifted a hand and rubbed it self-consciously.

'You're—' His eyes widened when they met hers, and she felt a rush of emotions from him. 'May I...?' His hand lifted of its own accord, towards her stomach, and Libby stood very still, her heart in her throat, everything going haywire.

'Of course,' she managed to say, her voice almost a whisper.

He closed his eyes as his hand connected with her stomach, his breath hissing out between his teeth, then his other hand lifted, feeling the other side of her belly, and she swayed a little because it was such a vital, important connection. Mother and father, their baby.

His eyes opened, locking to hers. Libby's heart stammered.

'Did you need something?'

She had meant it innocently. She'd meant it simply because he'd come to her room at ten o'clock, because he'd wanted to talk to her, but she heard the invitation in her words and knew she should say something to retract it. To pull away from him.

Desire was one thing, but Libby had to be stronger than this. She had to learn not to fall into a puddle every time he looked at her as though he wanted to peel her clothes from her body.

Except she didn't. Libby stood right there, blinking up at him, heart pounding, any semblance of resistance melting away in the face of her need for him.

'Libby,' he said darkly, angrily, and something in her chest hurt, but then his hand lifted higher on her side, holding her, and his throat shifted as he swallowed. Libby could only stare at him, as if drawn to him by a force so much greater than any she'd ever known. 'What is it about you?' he said with more anger, more darkness, and both of those emotions were palpable when he dropped his mouth to hers and kissed her as though the world would stop spinning if he didn't.

Libby swayed all the way forward then, pressing her body to his, a complete and willing surrender, not just to this moment but to something bigger, something inevitable and important. Lightning bolts flared inside her mind. She saw stars and felt heaven burst through her. It was nirvana; it was bliss, even when it was also terrifyingly complicated. A simple kiss yet it had the power to detonate something deep in her belly and all through her bones.

'Raul,' she groaned as she leaned closer to him, lifting a hand and curling it into the dark hair at the nape of his warm, strong neck. She felt him grow still. His whole body seemed to tense as though he were fighting something, perhaps the surge of need dominating them. Libby felt it and she refused to allow that fight; she had surrendered and needed him to as well. She kissed him and lifted one foot to the back of his calf, curving it around him, and it was like the unlocking of a door for both of them.

Raul cursed softly against her mouth and then he was moving, taking her with him, deeper into Libby's spacious bedroom, all the way to the king-size bed at its heart. They tumbled to the mattress together, arms, legs entwined, moving frantically now to remove each other's clothes, every touch, each brush of flesh incendiary and divine. Libby had never known anything like it...

Raul wanted to punch himself. No sooner had they exploded in unison, their bodies burning up in a fever of mutual desire, lust and need than he knew it had been a mistake. The whole thing. He lay beside her, a frown on his face, wishing he could take back the last twenty minutes, wishing he could erase their intimacy. For the look on Libby's face had been deeply troubling. Her eyes had softened, her lips had parted, and he'd felt something spark in his chest, something he instantly shied away from, something his brain knew to warn him off.

This was getting messy, and he didn't do mess. Not in his personal life. Not in any sector of his life, in fact. It made him want to run—to run as hard and fast as he could.

He pushed off her bed with an air of casual uncon- cern, swiped up his boxer shorts and pulled them on, then, when he had chosen a path of retreat, he steeled himself to turn and face Libby.

'I'm flying to Rome tomorrow.' His voice sounded odd to Libby, who was still floating high in the clouds of sensual euphoria after that magnificent coming together, so she didn't immediately understand what he'd said. She pressed a hand to her naked stomach on autopilot, frowning a little.

'I'm sorry?'

'I came here to tell you I'm going to Rome.' He crossed his arms over his chest, looking at her without a hint of emotion on his face.

Whatever glow Libby had been bathing in evaporated and she was suddenly ice-cold. As a child, she'd felt the sands shifting beneath her feet often. She knew nothing was permanent, no one was reliable. Everything could change at a moment's notice. Still, to go from making

love as though their lives depended upon it to…this…
felt like a kick in the guts.

'You did? You are?'

'I have a meeting.'

'Oh.' She felt like crying. She hated herself for feeling
that way, but her responses were innate. This wasn't just
Raul, it was every disappointment she'd known in her
life, it was a reminder of all the times she'd come home
to a 'new daddy', which meant the end of feeling, in some
small way, that she mattered to her mother. Change and
unpredictability were hardwired to invoke this response
in Libby; it was why she'd stayed single rather than dat-
ing men who might hurt her, why she'd been waiting for
her knight in shining armour to sweep in and love her—
love her in a way that would never, ever change.

She glanced down at the sheet, shielding her face
from Raul, desperately hoping he wouldn't see a hint of
the emotions she was fighting. 'Thanks…for letting me
know.' Her voice sounded hollow.

She was aware of him standing just inside the door
to her room, his clothes bunched in one hand. She felt
his eyes on her but didn't look up. She hardly breathed.

'If you need anything while I'm gone—'

'I won't,' she hastened to say.

'With the baby—' he clarified, and it was the worst
thing he could have said to Libby in that moment, because it served to remind her of the truth of their situation. She was simply an incubator to him. This wasn't
about her. Not as a person, a woman. Just as a womb.
She was stupid to have fallen back into bed with him, to
have so willingly given into—no, to have pushed him to
surrender to—the undercurrent of desire they both felt.

For all she knew, it was like this for Raul with every woman he slept with. Maybe the only reason they kept ending up in bed together was because she was simply *there*. Available, willing, in his apartment, under his nose. Mortifying thought.

She sucked in a deep breath. 'The baby is fine. I'm fine. Just…go to Rome.'

And then, just like that, he left.

Raul quickened his pace as he passed the Colosseum, barely noticing the beauty of the sun glancing across the ancient structure, the way the stones seemed to glow with gold in the early morning light. He kept his head down, moved faster, weaving around the few people who were on the streets, a Vespa parked across the kerb, a trash collector taking a cigarette break, then onto a busier section of footpath, with cafés set up for early morning patrons. He kept running until his lungs burned, but it didn't matter how fast he went, he couldn't wipe Libby from his mind. More specifically, the look in her eyes when he'd announced he was going to Rome.

It had been worse than he'd anticipated.

Her hurt and surprise were unmistakable.

He was so angry with himself. Not for leaving her to go on a business trip, but for allowing any of the lines between them to become blurred. Raul didn't *do* blurred lines, but there was something about Libby that had made him—temporarily—forget who he was, and how he lived. Except, perhaps it wasn't Libby. Maybe it was the baby instead, the fact that she had his child developing inside of her, that made him uncertain how to treat Libby.

What an idiot he'd been.

In trying to forge a connection with the woman, he'd inadvertently lied to her. He'd led her on. He'd let desire for her cloud his judgement, and now he was in the precarious situation of having to manage the emotions of a person who might very well have come to care for him.

Did she have any idea how stupid that was? What an unsafe person he was to let into her life? Not in a physical sense but emotionally, Raul was the last person in the world who could give Libby what she wanted.

And he had to make sure she understood that.

No more messing around, no more letting things get out of hand. Raul Ortega was married, but he needed his wife to understand that any kind of real relationship was—and always would be—out of the question.

CHAPTER ELEVEN

LIBBY WAS ON the second highest step of the ladder when she heard the door opening and she almost fell sideways, came disastrously close to knocking a half-full pot of paint onto the drop sheet below.

Her insides jolted alarmingly.

Five nights. Raul had been away the whole week and had not contacted her once.

But why would he have? she thought with self-directed anger. He didn't owe Libby anything, and he'd made it abundantly clear he couldn't wait to get away from her after that night.

Anger fired in her veins, a white-hot rage that might have been irrational, that might have been unfair, and yet it fairly exploded through her body. She ground her teeth together, dipped the brush into the tin and returned to the job at hand, carefully painting around the stencils she'd laboriously stuck in place. If he thought she was going to go out and acknowledge his return, he had another think coming.

Her fingers shook a little though as she continued with her work, one ear trained on the apartment, waiting for any indication that Raul was coming towards her. Minutes later, she heard it: the clicking open of the door to

this room, a sharp invective in his native language immediately following as he burst towards her like a hurricane.

'What the hell are you doing?'

Libby spun so fast she almost fell—again—but she
steadied herself quickly, shooting Raul an angry glare,
as though her clumsiness was his fault.

'What does it look like?' she muttered, hating how
good he looked, hating how her body immediately responded, and so turning away again quickly, focusing
back on the wall of the baby's nursery.

'It *looks*,' he said, with something very near derision
in his voice, 'like you have a death wish. Then again, I
should have known that from the first time we met and
you insisted on storming a boat.'

Libby jabbed the paintbrush angrily at the wall,
though it had done nothing to deserve such brutality.
'In case you'd forgotten, we're going to have a baby in a
few months. We need somewhere for that baby to sleep.'

'How could I forget, Libby? It's the reason we're married, isn't it?'

Libby's heart popped painfully. She jabbed the wall
again.

'Besides which,' he continued, voice deep and gruff
and closer than before, and when she happened to glance
down she saw he was standing at the base of the ladder,
one hand on the metallic rungs, 'we have many places
for the baby to sleep. Should you even be breathing that
stuff in?' he demanded.

His question *hurt*. As though he couldn't trust her to
keep their baby safe.

'It's non-toxic,' she snapped. 'I'm not an idiot. And I
don't have a death wish. I'm perfectly safe up here,' she

said, ignoring the couple of times she'd almost fallen in the last ten minutes. That had only been because of Raul's unexpected return. 'And your apartment might have many, many bedrooms but none of them is ready for a baby.'

Silence prickled between them, and Libby's anger was dangerously close to morphing into something else, something more like bitter sadness, so she ground her teeth and clung to her annoyance with Raul because it was so much safer than feeling sorry for herself.

'So hire a goddamned decorator,' he snapped.

'Why? I like doing it,' she said, mentally adding that she thought she'd done a good job, but to say as much to Raul might seem as though she was looking for his praise and she definitely wasn't.

'Because you can afford a decorator. Because they can do everything you want, without you risking a broken neck…'

'Far better for them to risk theirs,' she muttered, rolling her eyes. 'It's just a ladder.'

'Then let me do this,' he snapped.

'No.' She was being stubborn and churlish and she didn't care. Emotions were exploding through her, none of them good.

'You really are acting like a child,' he said, but stayed right where he was, one hand firmly gripping the base of the ladder, the other, she suspected, ready to swing into action and catch Libby if she should fall.

She ignored his jibe, continuing instead to paint the sunbeams on the wall, taking her time, refusing to show how unsettling his proximity was. Finally, she was at the end of her reach, and needed to shift the ladder.

'I'm coming down,' she said curtly, expecting him to move. And he did, but only slightly, just enough to make a little more room for Libby. Holding the tin of paint, she gingerly climbed down the treads of the ladder until her feet were on the ground, and then shifted sideways, as far away from Raul as a single step would take her. But here, at ground level, the flecks of anger in his eyes were so much more obvious, and they sparked an answering feeling in her bloodstream. Fire threatened to ravage her internal organs.

She looked away, mutinous.

'Are you finished?'

She pulled a face. 'Does it look finished?'

Raul's nostrils flared as he expelled a loud breath. 'What else?'

'Well, the sun has to go to that corner,' she snapped. 'If you want to help, go out of the room so I have more space to work.' It was a large bedroom and Raul was just a man, but he was a big man, and his presence was at least treble his size.

'Not on your life,' he responded coldly. 'Tell me what you want done, and I will do it.'

She gaped. 'I'm enjoying myself.'

'At great risk to our baby,' he responded pointedly and Libby's insides churned. He didn't care about her; this was all about the baby. And, worse, he thought she *didn't* care enough. He thought she was being reckless. Fear of being like her own mother flooded her; worry that she might be genetically incapable of doing this well gnawed at her. Tears filled Libby's eyes but she desperately didn't want him to see.

'Fine,' she said, bending down to replace the paint tin

on the ground rather than handing it to Raul and risking touching him. 'The sunbeams have to hit that corner. I'm going to make a tea,' she said, hands shaking as she ducked her head and left the room, her heart turning into something sharp and blade-like, slashing against the fibres of her chest wall.

'It's done.' His voice was without emotion ten minutes later when he strode into the lounge room. Libby was calmer now, the space from Raul and a cup of steaming hot tea were exactly what she'd needed to soothe her frazzled nerves. The reprieve was temporary. The moment he entered the spacious lounge, tension prickled along her spine.

She nodded curtly, didn't quite meet his eyes.

'Is there anything else?'

Her lips pulled to one side. 'Obviously.'

'Such as?'

Except Libby wasn't sure she wanted to confide in Raul. She'd chosen the nursery as her project the day after he'd left, when she'd known how important it was to stay busy and focus on something positive. The nursery had become her salvation—something she was tinkering with each day, thinking of their baby, the life inside of her, imagining a future with a little person who simply adored her.

'Nothing you need to worry about.'

He was quiet for so long that Libby felt her eyes pulling towards him, dragged there by the weight of his silence. His expression gave nothing away.

'Do you promise you will not go up the ladder again when I am not home?'

Libby's brows knit together. 'Um, no.'

'No, you will not go back up the ladder?'

'No, I don't promise any such thing,' she snapped. 'I'm not a moron, Raul, and, believe it or not, I care about our baby just as much as you do, or I wouldn't have agreed to go along with all this, would I?' she said, glad to be able to hurl that in his face, though she had no expectation of the sentiment proving as hurtful to Raul as it had been to her, particularly as it had come right after they'd just slept together.

'Then prove it. Don't do anything dangerous when you are alone in the apartment.'

'Going up a ladder is hardly—'

He held a hand up in the air, an instantly recognisable gesture of silence. Libby gawked at him. 'What if you had fallen?'

'I didn't.'

'You could have.'

'Then I would have called for help.'

'Who would you have called? In case you hadn't realised, this penthouse is somewhat isolated.'

She rolled her eyes. 'I have my phone in my back pocket.'

'And if you passed out?'

'You're talking in what-ifs. I could just as easily have slipped when I got out of the shower this morning, or rolled my ankle whilst making the bed…'

His eyes flashed to hers and his jaw tightened. 'You're right.' He crossed his arms over his chest. 'You should not be left alone.'

Libby's lips parted in surprise and her heart began to race. 'That's not what I meant.'

'But it's clear,' Raul contradicted. 'Until the baby is born, I'll work from home.'

Libby's face went whiter than a ghost's. 'N…no,' she stammered, rejecting the idea on some soul-deep level, even when she acknowledged there was a part of her that wanted his company and companionship. 'You're being ridiculous.'

'As ridiculous as a woman who thinks she has to carry a paperweight to protect someone like me from teenage tearaways?'

At the reminder of how they'd first met, Libby's pulse quickened. 'I'm not here all the time, Raul. I go out—a lot. Are you going to shadow me on the footpath too? Stop me from being hit by a bus or mugged in an alley?'

He ground his teeth. 'If that's necessary.'

Appalled, she glared at him. 'I was being sarcastic.'

'I wasn't.'

'But—'

'You are my *wife*.' He enunciated each word clearly. 'And the mother of my baby. Your safety is important to me.'

Libby spun away from him, hating herself for the way those words pulled at her, weakened her. 'Our baby's safety is important to me too,' she whispered, repeating something she'd already said, needing him to understand that she wasn't being reckless or careless. 'I am not taking stupid risks. I walk in busy areas in broad daylight. I never feel unsafe.'

'Nonetheless,' he said with his trademark authority, 'either I will come with you in the future or I'll arrange an escort.'

She stared at him as if he'd lost his mind. 'Like I'm

some kind of heroine in a Jane Austen novel?' she asked, scandalised. 'I'm a twenty-six-year-old woman,' she reminded him, 'and I've been looking after myself for longer than I can remember. Looking after everyone else too. If you think you can crash into my life like some kind of giant, arrogant wrecking ball and start taking over all of my...autonomy...and independence, then bloody think again.'

His features showed irritation. 'I have no interest in curtailing your autonomy, only in ensuring your safety.'

'They sound kind of the same, the way you describe them.'

'Then you're wilfully misunderstanding me.'

'I am not!' she responded with a disbelieving shake of her head. 'You are insufferable.'

'What a shame then that you have a lifetime to suffer me for.'

Libby dug her fingernails into her palms. A lifetime. It wouldn't be a lifetime and they both knew it, but it felt like it in that moment.

'Having regrets?' she asked, bracing her other hand against the kitchen bench.

'Regrets? I'm full of them,' he said, almost to himself, thrusting his hands on his hips with no idea how much his admission cut Libby to the very centre of her soul. 'But nothing changes our position now, does it? We're married, with a baby coming in a matter of months, and I am asking you, for the rest of your pregnancy, to remember you are making decisions for three people, not just one.'

Libby floundered. Her heart hurt. 'You don't need to remind me, Raul, I'm well aware of my pregnancy at every minute of every day. *You're* the one who's carrying on as though nothing has changed, whereas my entire life has been turned on its head from the moment you learned of this pregnancy...'

His eyes narrowed. 'You're right.' His agreement momentarily took the wind out of her sails. 'So I am telling you: my life is about to change too. From now on, I'll be here, with you. If you need a wall painted, I will do it. If you need furniture moved, ask me. You are not to do another job that involves even a hint of risk.'

'Everything involves risk,' she said on a frustrated laugh.

'Don't be argumentative for the sake of it,' he replied. 'You know some things carry greater risk, and scaling to virtually the top step of a ladder is one of them.'

She opened her mouth to say something, to dispute that, but slammed it shut again a moment later. Raul was right. There was an inherent risk in climbing up a ladder whilst alone in the apartment, and she'd known that. She'd been careful precisely for that reason.

She crossed her arms over her chest and glared at a point beyond his shoulder. 'Fine,' she said crisply. 'It's your life. Do whatever you want. But don't for one second think I need you here with me, Raul. I'm perfectly capable of getting through this pregnancy without your help and, news flash, I always was.' And with that she left the room.

A week later Libby felt as though she might burst.

Having Raul constantly around was like some kind of torture. He was *everywhere*. Working in the apartment from early in the morning until late at night, but frequently stepping into the lounge to check on her. If Libby wanted to go for a walk he came too, though he often worked then as well, using the time to make conference calls, so they were like two people on parallel paths, together yet apart. She had taken to walking two steps in front of him and doing her best to forget he was even there, or trying to at least, but Raul's presence was oppressive and overwhelming. Even several paces behind her, she *felt* him, and wished on a thousand stars she didn't.

But on their eighth day in this strange new form of hell, Libby came into the lounge room in the middle of the morning to find another woman standing just inside the apartment, a black leather briefcase clutched at her side, Raul in the process of greeting her.

Libby froze, frowning, wondering at the inclusion of someone else in their odd little arrangement.

'Libby.' Raul forced a smile, but there was a warning in his eyes. 'This is Matilda Roletti—a designer I've called to consult on the nursery. If you tell her what you'd like, she'll arrange it. And the installation.'

Libby's heart tightened and she frowned, because this was the last thing she wanted.

'Oh.' She glanced from Raul to Matilda, then back to Raul.

'I've brought some catalogues for us to look at, but perhaps you'd like to show me the space first?' Matilda spoke with a polished accent. In fact, everything about her was polished and professional and instantly intimidating to Libby, who felt under-dressed and dowdy in comparison. Having not been expecting company, she was dressed in just about the only clothes she owned that still fit—a pair of stretchy yoga pants and a loose T-shirt. She wore no make-up and her hair was long and fluffy around her face—Libby had given up on blow-drying it weeks ago.

'It's just over there.' She gestured to the nursery door—the bedroom beside her own. 'Why don't you go and have a look? I need a quick word with…my husband.'

Matilda nodded once then strode through the apartment with the same sense of belonging as the designer furniture. It was so obvious that Libby sucked in a sharp breath, the sting in the middle of her chest almost felling her. *This* was the kind of woman who belonged in Raul's home. This was the kind of woman who would have been comfortable and content amongst Raul's priceless collection of furniture in his incredibly extravagant penthouse. Not Libby Langham, a cleaner from Sydney. She swallowed past the constricting feeling in her throat.

'What do you think you're doing?' She rounded on him, hissing the question in a whisper, but her anger reverberated around the room as though she'd shouted. 'I don't need a designer.'

'You said you wanted the nursery to be done.'

'No, I said I wanted to do it,' she responded.

'So you can. Choose what you want with Matilda…'

'That's not what I meant.' Libby groaned. 'God, Raul, you are unbelievable.'

'What have I done wrong?' he disputed with disbelief. 'I'm trying to help.'

'No, you're trying to take over and do things your way, which I'm starting to realise means with an abundance of money and no actual time or feeling.'

The words slammed into the space between them,

heavy with accusation and accuracy. She saw him rock back on his heels as though it was the last thing he'd expected her to recognise or say, but Libby didn't apologise nor take the words back. It was true.

'I just hope that when our baby is born you realise they're going to want to spend time with you, not just live in your sky palace and benefit from your fabulous wealth.'

'You think I don't know that?' Raul responded, suddenly pale beneath his tan. 'You think I didn't realise that the moment you told me about the pregnancy? If I wanted to spend money and be done with this, I would have set up a trust fund for the baby and walked away.'

Libby angled her face away from Raul's.

'I am going to be in this baby's life,' he said, the words low and deep but carefully muted of emotion.

It's why I married you.

Raul didn't need to say it again: the refrain was etched in Libby's mind.

'And haven't I been spending time with you?'

It was like waving a red flag in front of a bull.

'You've been shadowing me! That's not spending time together.'

He thrust his hands on his hips. 'I don't know what you want from me, Libby. I really don't.'

She turned away, angry and frustrated. She didn't know either. That was part of the problem. But, deep down, Libby felt like this was all wrong. Everything Raul did seemed to make it worse.

She clung to belligerence, not wanting to back down. Her unreliable pregnancy emotions were zipping all over the place; she felt robbed of her usual optimism and self-control. 'I don't want a decorator.'

There was silence for a moment and when Raul spoke his voice was level, but that didn't matter. Libby heard his frustration, heard his impatience. 'You don't even want to meet with her, to hear her ideas?'

'I have my own ideas,' Libby said quietly. 'I've had plenty of time to think about what I want our baby's room to be like, and it's nothing, *nothing*, like this ice-scape.' She waved her hand around the lounge room, the impersonal, cold furniture anathema to Libby's sense of warmth and family. '*You* go and hear her thoughts,' Libby snapped. 'I'm sure you'll be a match made in heaven.'

It took him five minutes to dismiss Matilda and he did so without embarrassment, mainly because Raul didn't feel those emotions in the normal course of his life, and for the moment his mind was singularly engaged in decoding and understanding Libby, so he had very little run time to feel something as pedestrian as embarrassment. Besides, he would no doubt get an invoice for the designer's time, even when the visit had been totally unproductive.

Alone once more in the apartment with Libby, he knew the right thing—the wise thing—to do was give her space, and so he returned to his own work, fuming over how unreasonable she'd been, staring at his screen with the sense of a spring being wound tighter and tighter in his belly.

But no matter how frustrated he was with Libby, he still found it impossible to stop thinking about her, and to ignore the feeling that they'd got halfway through an argument they needed to finish properly. Yes, that was it, he thought on a wave of relief. They had unfinished business and for this reason, and this reason alone, he wanted to go to her, to pick up where they'd left off. Until they'd resolved this dispute, he wasn't sure he'd be able to concentrate anyway, so there was no sense in just staring at a blank screen.

He found her in the nursery, one shoulder propped against the wall, eyes trained on the view beyond the window. He stood just inside the door, arms crossed, watching her, suddenly at a loss for words. Her blonde hair again reminded him of an angel's halo, her eyes were sparkling like gems.

'I'm sorry.'

Raul was still searching for what to say, so Libby's softly voiced apology caught him off-guard.

She turned to face him slowly. 'I overreacted.'

He frowned, taking a step deeper into the room and then another, until he was just a short distance from her.

Libby's gaze probed his, as if looking for something important, then she sighed. 'When I was growing up, my room was just a mattress on the floor in a space no bigger than a wardrobe.' Her lips pulled to the side in that way she had; Raul knew it meant she was lost in thought. 'I know neither of us planned for this,' she said, rubbing her stomach distractedly. 'But, at the same time, I've planned for it all my life. As a young girl, I used to imagine what my house would be like, my bedroom, if only I could have it my way. As a teenager, I imagined my future, my family, and from the moment I found out I was pregnant, I've thought about how to make this baby's life everything mine wasn't. It's not about possessions,' she clarified quickly. 'It's about warmth. Security. Love.'

Something tightened in Raul's chest.

He would give their baby the world, but love was the one thing he knew he couldn't offer. Not to the baby, not to Libby, not to anyone. He'd lost that ability a long time ago, and it was something he never wanted to regain.

Fortunately, Raul had no doubt Libby would love their child enough for the both of them, and he would provide everything else that was needed in spades.

'I was trying to help,' he said gruffly, rather than admitting the truth to Libby about the deadened state of his heart.

'I know that, and I appreciate it. But this is what I want to do for our baby. It's important to me, and I enjoy it.'

His gaze moved from Libby to the walls of the room, seeing it with renewed interest. On one side she'd painted a circus theme—a big, bright tent with a waving flag on top, an elephant and a happy clown with a rainbow bursting out of the palm of his hand across another wall, then, on the other, it was a sky theme, with clouds and a gloriously bright sun. Not only was it cheery and warm, it was well executed, so Raul's eyes shone with approval when they met Libby's.

'You're very talented.'

She laughed softly. 'You sound surprised.'

He lifted one hand in the air in apology, and found his lips lifting in an unexpected grin. 'I shouldn't be. You're clearly a woman of many talents.'

She scrutinised the artwork on one wall. 'I drew the outline with pencil first, until I was happy.'

He tried not to think about how many times she'd been up and down the ladder in the week he'd been away.

'I know what I want to do in here, Raul. I was just waiting until you got back in case...'

Her voice trailed off into nothing and his gut tightened in anticipation of what she was going to say. 'I thought you might want to be involved in selecting the furniture,' she said with a shrug. 'But you don't have to. I can do it myself.'

Good. That was the wise choice. She should do it herself.

Raul had to forcibly remind himself of the importance of keeping those lines clear, their boundaries delineated. The less time they spent doing happy family-type activities, the better.

He nodded once. 'I look forward to seeing what you pick out. I presume you can order the necessary items online?'

He ignored the look of hurt in her eyes with difficulty.

She bit into her lip as she nodded. 'I'll get it delivered next week.'

CHAPTER TWELVE

SOME OF THE pieces Libby had selected for the nursery were coming from Europe, and so it took almost a month for everything to arrive. She left each item in its box until the last piece was in the apartment, and by the time that had happened her stomach had become so round it was difficult to get up and down off the floor to do anything, let alone assemble furniture. She and Raul had developed an excellent routine for living in the same space whilst more or less ignoring one another—or at least appearing to.

For Libby, it had become a form of torture. How could she ignore someone who was so intrinsic to the air she breathed? His presence was so overpowering, so overwhelming, he was simply *everywhere*. Not just in the apartment, but in her mind, her thoughts, her dreams. It was truly frustrating because they both treated one another like polite strangers.

Even when he accompanied her to medical appointments, he was more like a chaperone than an expectant father, and misgivings had begun to form in the back of Libby's mind. Doubts. Worries.

What if he was regretting his hasty decision to marry

her? What if he was regretting his insistence on being in the baby's life?

It had all happened so fast there hadn't been time for regrets, but now that the dust had settled and he was faced with the reality of living with Libby—and the impending arrival of their baby—he might very well be wishing things were different.

She'd caught him staring at her several times, frowning, his expression unreadable except for the fact he was obviously thinking *something*—and something that didn't bring him much pleasure. His eyes often fell to her belly—too big to ignore now. Libby had been forced to buy some maternity clothes, and even those were feeling a little tight already.

Twisting the wrench, her hand slipped and the tool fell to the ground, hitting her hard on the ankle.

'Damn it,' she cursed loudly, rubbing the flesh, instinctive tears filling her eyes. She'd been louder than she'd intended, and it brought Raul to the door of the nursery.

When he saw the destruction in there, she realised he hadn't been in the place for weeks. Not since the day of the designer, when she'd apologised to him for overreacting. Almost as if he'd been ignoring the nursery?

'What the hell happened in here?'

She stared at him. 'What does it look like?' She rubbed her ankle. His eyes dropped to the gesture, then he crossed the room, crouching in front of her so his jeans pulled against his haunches, and something powerful ignited in her bloodstream. A desire she'd been trying to ignore, to fight, because he'd made it clear he didn't feel that way about her any more. He hadn't even been close enough to touch her in over a month. So much for being friends. At this stage, she'd have settled for a conversation that didn't feel so stilted it hurt.

'It looks like a bomb went off,' he admitted. 'May I?' His hand hovered close to her ankle but without touching. Libby was terrified that if his fingers pressed to her skin she might actually explode.

'I'm fine,' she demurred, moving away from him a little, standing with a total lack of elegance and rubbing her belly, then her neck, surveying the room and seeing it as he must have. In one corner, she'd stacked a heap of cardboard packaging. She'd managed to assemble the changing table and was halfway through the crib.

'Libby—' he stood too, moving closer to her; she caught a hint of his cologne and her insides trembled '—why didn't you order these things assembled?'

Heat rushed to her cheeks. 'It cost extra.'

Raul didn't laugh, and she was grateful for that, but she felt his disapproval. She knew how stupid she'd been. He was one of the wealthiest people in the world—as if he would have balked at the additional expense of pre-assembled furniture.

'I needed something to do,' she added defensively. 'I thought it would be easier than this. I've… I've never had anything new before.' She lifted her shoulders. 'I had no idea.'

Raul's voice was gruff. 'Why didn't you ask me for help?'

Libby looked across at him, frowning. 'We've hardly been speaking,' she pointed out. 'I didn't feel like I could.'

His eyes flashed with an emotion she didn't understand. 'I thought space was a good idea for both of us, but you need to know that you can always come to me for help, Libby. You're my wife.'

She pulled a face. 'Yeah, right.'

'What is that supposed to mean?'

'I'm your wife in name only,' she pointed out. 'It's not a real marriage, and we both know that.'

'It's real for us, for our version of marriage.'

That hurt, because he was right. Their marriage wasn't what Libby had wanted, it wasn't what she'd imagined, but it was what she'd agreed to. She nodded awkwardly.

'Pass me the wrench,' he said, holding out his hand.

'You don't have to do this.'

His eyes pinned her to the spot. 'Yes, I do.' Then, after a beat, 'I want to.'

Libby passed the tool over with a massive wave of relief.

It was much easier watching Raul work than doing the work herself, she thought with a grimace ten minutes later as he took over the assembly of the crib with a seeming lack of effort that stole her breath.

He worked for almost an hour and then it was done, but Raul wasn't finished. 'What's next?'

Libby stared at the crib, her heart twisting in her chest. 'It's perfect,' she whispered, putting a hand on the edge of it, tears in her eyes. And it was at that moment, that *exact* moment, that their baby shifted and kicked and Libby gasped, because it was so different to the other movements she'd felt—which had been more like gentle popping sensations. This was a rollercoaster in her belly.

'What is it?' Raul was instantly concerned.

Libby was so overcome by the magic of the moment she didn't stop to question the wisdom of what she was doing; she simply reached out for Raul's hand and pressed it to her stomach, eyes wide as the baby once more flipped and kicked, this time, right against Raul's palm.

It was Raul's turn to react, his expression assuming a mask of shock, his lips parting on an exhalation, his eyes hooded, focused on Libby's stomach.

'That is our baby,' he said, shaking his head as he lifted his other hand to Libby's stomach and held it there. More somersaults.

They stared at one another and then Libby was laughing, and also sobbing, the emotion of the moment overpowering her, even before Raul lifted one hand to her cheek and held her still, his eyes locked to hers.

'That's our baby,' he repeated, and then he dropped his head, pressing his forehead to hers. Libby closed her eyes, swallowing past a wave of emotion, everything inside of her rolling and twisting so she lost sight of who and where she was.

Instincts overrode everything, just as they had on the boat.

She was an animal, acting solely on biological impulses. She tilted her head, her lips seeking his and finding them, taking them, kissing him lightly at first, curiously, and then hungrily, desperately, needily, and it was a need that only intensified when he kissed her back, his mouth claiming hers with all the heat of possessiveness he'd shown her in the past.

She didn't think. Didn't wonder. Didn't question.

It was too perfect: too right.

Everything inside Libby ignited on a cloud of intense pleasure. Heat built between her legs; her breasts tingled with a need for him to touch them. She was on fire in the best possible way.

'God, Raul,' she groaned into his mouth. 'I want you.' His hand pushed into her hair, fingers tangling in its length as he held her head where it was, against his mouth, his tongue duelling with hers, and Libby said, over and over, 'Yes, yes,' until she was incandescent, her body pressing against his, her hands clasped behind his back, holding him to her. She was exploding with feelings, too many feelings to understand, but they were oh, so powerful and saturating.

In the back of her mind there was a warning bell, but she couldn't hear it, let alone heed it, or perhaps it was just that she didn't want to. After a month of walking on eggshells, being utterly ignored, it felt so good to stand face to face with their desire once more, to know that the heat responsible for initially bringing them together was still a force neither could fully resist.

It was the only thing about their marriage that made any kind of sense.

Until it didn't.

Suddenly Raul was very still, and then he was pulling back, lifting his head and staring at Libby with dazed surprise, dropping his hands from her head, her body, as though she were a scorching-hot potato, staring at his fingers like he didn't recognise them.

'That shouldn't have happened,' he said with self-directed anger.

Libby's stomach rolled and dropped to her toes. She didn't trust herself to speak at first.

'It was feeling the baby move,' he explained stilt-edly, then took a step backwards. 'I wasn't prepared.' A frown furrowed his brow. 'I'll finish the furniture to-night, once you are in bed. Don't trouble yourself with it further, Libby.' He moved to the door and then, in a last insult, nodded his head in a businesslike fashion be-fore departing.

Libby stared at the space he'd just occupied, her lips still heavy from the pressure of his, and then she closed her eyes on a wave of desperation.

The emotions inside of her were still hard to under-stand, but more and more she was starting to fear one of them in particular—an emotion it would be truly awful to feel for her husband. Was it possible that, despite ev-erything, she'd actually been stupid enough to fall in love with him?

Raul couldn't outrun it, not this time. He went faster, harder, the treadmill of his home gym no substitute for the open streets, but at least here he was around should Libby need him.

I need you.

Not *that* kind of need.

But even remembering the soft, desperate way she'd called to him did something strange to his gut, so he had to work hard to stay focused on the rhythm of his steps, one foot after the other. He increased the incline, want-ing to sweat, to hurt—to hurt so much he could no lon-ger think, feel, remember.

Flashes sliced through him—other memories, those he tried hardest of all to blank. They were a talisman now, a reminder of why he was the way he was, the self-protective instincts that had served him well since boyhood.

Rejection after rejection. Hurt after hurt—some physical, like being smacked repeatedly by one of his foster parents for coming home with a torn school shirt. Some emotional, like being told he was a waste of skin, that he'd never amount to anything. Being told that no one would ever want him. The last one had been easiest of all to believe.

He ground his teeth, closing his eyes for a moment, hating the memories, hating the experiences most of all, but grateful he'd learned to be truly independent from a young age. By the time he was thirteen, no one had held the power to hurt him. He simply didn't let anyone in.

The closest he'd come was Maria and Pedro and, even then, it had been about making them proud, not letting them love him. Certainly not loving them back.

I need you.

He didn't *want* to be needed, but it was marginally better than his needing anyone else. Raul was determined never to weaken in that regard. He was forged from steel—from rejection, hurt, wounds that had cut him so deeply he'd sworn he'd never allow anyone to cut him again. He was strong now. Physically, mentally, emotionally.

Libby was simply another person in his universe, but she would never have the power to hurt him. He refused to give it to her.

Libby woke early and dressed silently, creeping from her room in what she only acknowledged was an attempt to evade Raul when she reached the front door and slipped her feet into her boots.

He'd been her shadow for a long time, and she'd tolerated it. But yesterday, in the nursery, something inside of her had snapped. Kissing him as though her life depended on it and having Raul back away had been a death knell to her ability to pretend any longer.

He wasn't just the father of her baby. He wasn't simply a man she'd married because of the pregnancy.

He was Raul Ortega and somewhere, somehow, everything had got muddled. Libby wanted more from him. More than a marriage of convenience, more than a businesslike partnership. More than friendship.

Deep down, she was still that little girl who believed in fairy tales and soulmates, and suddenly it seemed possible, if not likely, that everything they'd experienced had been for exactly that simple reason—destiny.

What if they were destined to find one another?

Two people who'd been broken in different ways by their broken childhoods. Who'd known hurt, loss, pain, rejection and fear as kids, who'd fought hard to find their feet as adults, who were now determined to give their own child the best of everything, because they'd never known it.

What if Libby possessed, within herself, everything she needed to heal Raul, and the same was true in reverse? What if they could just be open to that possibility?

Her breath snagged in her throat as she pressed the button for the lift, waiting for it to appear with her fingers crossed, because she didn't want to see Raul yet. She wasn't ready. She needed to think, and for that she required space. She needed to process and understand her feelings, to comprehend the sensations that were expanding inside of her.

The lift doors opened and she stepped through them with gratitude, pressed her back to the wall and then sighed a big breath of relief when they silently zipped shut.

Downstairs and on the corner of the block, she ordered a coffee—her one pregnancy indulgence, which she allowed herself to enjoy only once per day—with caramel syrup, wrapped her hands around the cup then took a sip as she left the café, looking left and right.

It was a beautiful morning, the weather turning incrementally warmer, and she longed to explore the city in all its guises, but especially spring. Trees were beginning to show their first bloom of leaves and blossom. Her mind turned longingly to Central Park, and the beauty she knew she'd find there as things began to grow again. Though winter had also been stunning, with the snow-covered ground and eerie, spindly trees almost seeming to scrape long tendrils of fingers against the leaden sky.

She walked without purpose or destination, simply to move, and with walking came thoughts and clarity, even when she didn't intentionally seek either. It had always been that way for Libby—a walk somehow unlocked things within her.

Each step seemed to cement something, an idea, a concept, that had begun so long ago, and so incrementally, she couldn't even say for sure when the idea had first occurred to her. Not consciously ever but, looking back, she supposed she'd felt a red flag very early on. Perhaps even on the boat, when Raul had suggested dinner. Libby had balked then, because he'd been so *every-*

thing, and she hadn't known quite how to handle that. Or maybe it had been even earlier, when she'd insisted on going with him to confront the boat thieves, as if she'd known that she had to defend him, to protect him, because even when they were total strangers, the idea of anything happening to Raul had been unimaginable.

And then she'd found out about the baby and she'd felt the first rush of love. Unmistakable and all-consuming, it had made her fingertips tingle with possibility and hope. Of course she'd loved her baby, but had it been more than that? Had she loved, even then, the idea of Raul too? Of growing a person who was half him? Of the certainty she would get to know Raul, even if only through their child?

She ran a hand over her stomach, patting the baby distractedly, connecting with that little lifeform, silently promising them the world, as she did all the time.

Libby had always wanted the fairy tale. The dream. But she'd come to accept it might not be possible.

But what if it was?

What if the answer, her hopes, her heart's desire, had been staring her in the face this whole time, and she'd been too shell-shocked to understand? Too stubborn, too *scared* to admit that the pragmatic terms they'd negotiated were just a shield they were both using to protect themselves from any possible fallout?

Libby stopped walking and stared straight ahead. It was early enough in the morning that the street was still quiet, but even if the sidewalk had been brimming with people, she wouldn't have been capable of noticing.

Her breath caught in her throat and she clicked her

fingers in the air, the answer seeming so bloody obvious to her now.

They were both scared. They were both using the terms of their arrangement as a shield.

Whenever they got close to breaking through that shield, Raul pulled back, reminding her forcibly of what they were, because he couldn't accept a reality in which he cared for Libby as a person.

She groaned softly and turned on her heel, walking with renewed purpose back to their apartment, a smile tingling the corners of her mouth even when her tummy was tied in a thousand, billion knots with nervousness at the conversation in her near future. It was the only way to move forward, and suddenly she was convinced she could do this.

If fate had brought them together, and she knew in her heart that it had, it was Libby's job to listen—and to make sure Raul did too.

'Come on, baby.' She smiled at the doorman as she returned to Raul's building. 'Let's go tell your daddy how much we love him and just see if he doesn't feel the same way.'

CHAPTER THIRTEEN

RAUL WAS IN the kitchen when Libby returned to the apartment, a cup of coffee in one hand, a large tablet in front of him with one of the daily newspapers on the screen.

He frowned. 'You've been out?'

She stepped out of her boots, then removed her denim jacket, carrying it over one arm. 'I went for a walk.' She held up her coffee as if that explained everything.

'You should have told me,' he said with obvious disapproval. 'I would have come with you.'

She stared at him as if up was somehow down, because it was, in so many ways. An abstract concept whilst walking outside, face to face with Raul now, she had to accept that yes, she absolutely did love him. And that this conversation, while necessary, was the most important of her life.

It was also the most terrifying.

Every time her mother had let a new man move in, Libby had known rejection. She'd lost her mother, not once, not twice, but again and again and again. She'd always been second-best. A consolation prize when her mother was single. Nothing more. She'd never been important, really important, to anyone.

What if she wasn't important to Raul? Could she take that rejection?

Uncertainty pierced the veil of hope that had begun to shroud her; she fidgeted with her fingers.

But Libby had learned to lean into optimism. Perhaps it had been her earliest and best survival skill, a form of delusion even, to hope when hope seemed stupid. She saw beauty, sunlight, brightness, because it had helped her survive the emotionally barren nature of her upbringing, and she saw hope now, even against the odds.

Fate had brought them here; Libby was sure of it.

'I needed to think,' she said honestly, taking a few steps closer, pausing on the other side of the kitchen counter. It was like waking up from a dream, seeing everything for the first time.

This apartment was impersonally furnished, but it was beautiful and she realised she'd been wrong about this too, because it had absolutely come to feel like home. She belonged here. Maybe it wasn't about the picket fence and flowerbeds and cosy furnishings, but about who you were with…

She stared at Raul with a sense of wonder, a sense of dawning comprehension, and she smiled, despite the nerves that were making her stomach loop and twist.

'You look happy.' Raul, in contrast, seemed perplexed.

'Do I?' She bit down on her lower lip. 'I think I am. Or I might be. I don't know. That's kind of up to you, I guess.' She shook her head, because that was the wrong thing to have said. She didn't want to pressure Raul into thinking he had to return her feelings. As if anyone could pressure Raul into anything! But this had to be an act of choice, a decision they both made, if it was ever going to work.

'Is it?'

His cautious tone caused her confidence, and mood, to dip slightly.

'Raul, about yesterday…'

'It was a mistake.' A muscle pulsed low in his jaw. 'I apologise.'

'But what if it wasn't,' she said quickly, the words rushing out of her. 'What if it was the right thing to do?'

His expression was impossible to interpret, but she saw the immediate rejection in the depths of his eyes and it stung, way more than she'd expected. This was going to be hard.

'It wasn't.'

'Why not?'

'Our situation is complicated enough without letting sex enter the equation.'

'Sex *is* a part of our equation,' she reminded him. 'It's disingenuous to pretend otherwise.'

'We can control that.'

'Evidently not,' she said, patting her stomach.

'From now on.'

'Why?'

He looked at her as though she'd started speaking a made-up language.

'Why do we have to control how we feel?' she pushed. 'Why can't we just surrender to what's good in this relationship? And there is so much good, Raul. In fact, I think this could be one of the best things either of us has ever done.'

He looked stricken. 'It was a mistake,' he repeated.

'It was a kiss.'

He shook his head. 'Not yesterday. This.' He gestured to Libby's stomach. 'The boat. Sex. The pregnancy. None of this was supposed to happen.'

She ignored the immediate inflection of pain, held true to her goal in having this conversation, but a part of Libby was falling through the cracks in time, becoming a little girl again, desperate to put her heart on the line because she knew no one loved her.

'But it did. We slept together because neither of us could resist.'

'We had been through something. Adrenalin is a powerful motivator.'

'It wasn't just adrenalin. It was a feeling that if I didn't reach out and grab you, I'd always regret it. How much I wanted you scared the heck out of me. It's why I said no to dinner that night.' She leaned closer, putting her hand on his. 'It's why you asked me for dinner. Isn't it?'

Something shifted in the very depths of his eyes, but he blanked whatever emotion he'd been feeling almost immediately.

'I asked you for dinner because it seemed appropriate, given we'd just had sex. I didn't want you to feel used.'

Her stomach tightened. Was that true? Had it just been a case of going through the motions for Raul?

'I don't believe you,' she said, shaking her head.

'That's your prerogative.'

She flinched. His coldness was worse than anything.

'It didn't mean anything,' he continued in the same tone. 'And if our baby hadn't been conceived, we would never have seen one another again.'

Libby's heart seemed to disconnect from her body.

She stared at him in surprise. Surprise that he could say that so calmly, surprised at the version of the world he painted, surprised that the idea of not having Libby in his life didn't bother him at all.

But then surprise faded to understanding. No one had loved her when she was young, and no one loved her now.

Libby's throat felt thick with unshed tears. She'd been wrong. Not about her feelings, but about the likelihood of Raul returning them.

She had been about to confess something that would make their whole marriage untenable. Worse, it would have made him feel *pity* for her. He was already treating her with kid gloves, acting as though he needed to walk on eggshells around her. Admitting that she'd fallen in love with him would have made that a thousand times worse.

'You're probably right,' she said, shivering, the words trembling a little as she accepted his responses for what they were. Rejection. Even without telling him she loved him, Raul was making his feelings clear.

Libby swallowed past a lump in her throat, tried to force herself to smile but couldn't quite manage it.

'I'm going to be in the nursery.' She spun away from him, almost spilling her coffee in the hasty manner of her departure. 'See you later.'

Everything was perfect, she thought, turning slowly to admire the room, a hand on her stomach connecting her to the baby that all this effort had been for. From the brightly coloured walls to the sleek minimalist furnishings and happy, pale yellow bedlinen, the room was set up for its future occupant in a way that made Libby's spirits lift. At least a little. It was solace. Somewhere to go to remember why she was doing this. To remind herself that things were okay. Everything would be fine.

She could live with this equation. She could live with one part of her life being great—their baby. In fact, it was more than just one part, she reminded herself with a degree of forced optimism. She had things she'd never known existed. She had the kind of financial stability that would allow her to pursue whatever dreams she chose. *Our marriage can give you wings.* She closed her eyes on a shuddery breath, memories of Raul, his promises, making her skin tingle.

Libby had always been determined to see the goodness in life. To give the darkness perspective and make it tolerable. But suddenly she wasn't sure it would be enough.

The idea of living with Raul, of loving him and getting only a limited part of him in return—those parts he was amenable to sharing—made her chest feel as though a whole ton of cement had been dropped onto it. She didn't just want parts of him; she wanted *all* of him.

She wanted him. The real him, flaws, vulnerabilities, everything.

He had to know that, she realised, eyes widening.

For all that Libby's childhood had shaped her, his had too. When was the last time someone had said they loved him and meant it? When was the last time someone had told him he could be broken and imperfect and it wouldn't matter because they accepted him for who he was? She spun quickly, legs carrying her from the nursery before she could question her decision. And even if she were to question it, nothing would change, because she was right. She knew she was right.

No matter how he reacted, no matter what he said he felt, he needed to hear this.

He was still standing at the kitchen bench when she returned, coffee refreshed, newspaper on the tablet lit up. Her heart thumped against her ribs. She loved him. Suddenly the idea of *not* being able to tell him was anathema to Libby. Come what may, she had to do this.

'I wasn't finished,' she said breathily, coming to stand right beside him, taking comfort and strength from his nearness.

He placed his coffee down on the bench, tilted his face towards hers. There was resignation in his eyes and defensiveness in the tight set of his features. Libby ignored both.

'I know neither of us planned this. I'm not an idiot. Look at who we are, our lives, the way we live—our paths would never normally have crossed. In what world would someone like you even look at someone like me?' she said, missing the way his eyes narrowed and his lips parted, as though he was about to say something. 'Sleeping together wasn't planned, but it wasn't a mistake. And even without this baby, I think we both would have wanted to see one another again.'

His eyes were shuttered, totally inaccessible.

'Did you think of me, after that night?' she pushed, her breath held, her stomach trembling with fear.

Raul's throat shifted. 'Does it matter?'

'Did you think of me?' she persisted.

'I think of lots of things, people, all the time. It doesn't mean anything.'

Libby's smile was sad. 'That's your refrain for everything,' she murmured. 'You think you can cling to the idea that nothing matters and you'll be safe from getting hurt again. But I don't care how many times you say that, it's not true. Not with me.'

He flinched but Libby was on a roll.

'Yes, I see you, Raul. I understand you, maybe better than anyone ever has, because in so many ways we're the same. We've been through the same rejection. The same insecurity as children. The same holes in our lives where loving parents should be.'

'We are not the same.' He spoke quietly, calmly. 'Were you beaten by foster parents, Libby, for having the temerity to watch television after school? Were you told that the world would be better without you? Not just by one family, but in different ways by each family you were sent to live with, until it became the refrain you heard each night as you fell asleep?'

She closed her eyes on a wave of grief that threatened to envelop her. 'I wish I could take those things away from you,' she said. 'I wish they'd never happened. It's all so wrong.' Tears sparkled on her lashes. 'But Raul, that's why I have to say this, and I know it's not what you want to hear, but you *need* to hear it anyway. I love you.'

He closed his eyes, his nostrils flaring, but Libby carried on. She'd known this would be hard, but it was vitally important. Even when she was terrified, loving someone meant going out on a limb and for Raul she would do that.

'I—' she paused, enunciating each word '—love—'

her hand lifted to his chest, fingers splayed wide '—you. All of you, just as you are. I see value in you, strength, kindness, goodness. You are important, and worthy of being loved, of being part of this family. I love you.'

'Stop.' He reached for her hand, put his over it, his eyes boring into hers. 'Just stop.'

She shook her head. She'd expected resistance. She knew he might never be able to accept her love, but that didn't stop her from wanting to say this, to tell him how she felt.

'Why?' She took a step closer. 'Because you're scared to let me love you? Because you're scared to let anyone close?'

'I have been honest with you from the beginning, haven't I?' There was a plea in his voice. 'This wasn't about love. Not ever.'

'It was always about love,' she contradicted. 'I've never really believed in things like fate and destiny. They seem like such dangerous concepts to me. The idea of leaving the happiness of your future in the hands of unseen, intangible forces—how crazy. We make our own futures, our own happiness, our own destiny. But how can either of us deny that fate had a hand in this? I have only slept with one other person, Raul, and that was years before I met you. I'm not someone who has casual sex with strangers, but it never felt like that with you. I didn't understand it at the time, it's only looking back that I can see things with clarity. From the moment we met, I knew you were different. Important somehow. Right from the beginning. Tell me you didn't feel the same about me,' she challenged, then immediately wished she could take the words back, because she desperately didn't want to hear any such thing from his perfect, beautiful mouth.

Yet she stayed the course. Brave in the face of fear, confident in her love being enough to overcome anything.

'I didn't,' he said, but quietly, gently, as though he didn't want to hurt her. 'I don't.'

Her heart cracked but she didn't flinch outwardly. 'You're afraid.'

His eyes flexed. 'Am I?'

'You might not want to admit it, but yes, of course you are. In here—' she drummed her fingers against his chest '—you're still the same little boy who was hurt over and over again and you're scared that if you let me love you, I'll hurt you too.'

'Damn it, Libby.' She'd hit a nerve. He took a step back, dropping her hand, putting space between them, his back ramrod straight. 'Don't act as though you understand me.'

'I do understand you though, Raul, and I love you.'

'Stop saying that,' he demanded, raking his fingers through his hair. 'This is not what we agreed.'

'Yeah, well, I've got news for you, buster. Life doesn't always go to plan. Remember? We've said that before. I didn't know I loved you when we started doing this, but I know now, and I want you to know it too.'

'Why?' he asked, looking at her as if truly, desperately searching for answers. 'Why do I need to know any of this? It changes nothing.'

Her smile was sad, wistful, but she didn't shy away from this conversation.

'Maybe not today,' she said with a lift of one shoulder. 'Maybe not tomorrow, or in a month, but eventually, when you get used to how much our child and I love you, to the fact we're not going anywhere, that there's nothing you can do that will make us love you less, it will change *everything*. One day, you'll wake up and see yourself as I do, you'll see that you're worthy of being loved. That you can accept it, welcome it, maybe even return it.'

'No.' The word was cutting, spoken quickly, an instant rejection. 'It's not possible.'

'How do you know?' she asked, her throat feeling thick, making it hard to swallow.

'Because this is a choice, Libby. I have chosen to live like this.'

'A life without love?'

'A life without vulnerability and weakness,' he corrected. 'The kind of feeling you're talking about is the opposite of everything I want. I refuse to allow it.'

'You can't refuse to allow me to love you,' she said. 'That's preposterous.'

'But I can refuse to be affected by your love, refuse to be changed by it. I don't want to change. I'm happy as I am.'

'Liar,' she said with a firm shake of her head.

'This is what I want,' he said emphatically. 'I am in control. I depend on no one.'

'What about when our baby is born?' she said, taking a step closer to him, then pausing when he stiffened, obviously not welcoming any contact. He didn't respond, simply looked at Libby with a question in his eyes, so she shook her head gently. 'You don't think you're going to love him or her? That you'll be vulnerable and dependent on how much you adore our child?'

Raul's expression didn't soften. If anything, it grew more determined, more stubborn. 'I will give our baby everything necessary.'

Something shifted inside Libby. 'You'll love our baby.'

'There are other things that matter just as much as love.'

Libby stared at him, her heart slamming through her body. 'Not to a child,' she murmured.

'You will love our baby,' he said, softly though, as if needing to convince himself of this path. 'You will love our baby so much they will never doubt their value and worth. You will fill their heart and soul with belonging.'

'And what will you do?' she asked.

'I'll be here.' The words were dragged out of him, and Libby felt only sadness then for this big alpha guy who'd been so badly shattered by his childhood. 'I will support our child, encourage them, be in their life. That has to be enough—for both of you.'

Libby's eyes swept shut. 'You won't even let yourself love this baby, will you?'

'Does it matter?' The words were bleak.

'Do you really think so little of yourself?' she said with sad acceptance in her tone. 'You don't think it matters that you will be in our baby's life and not love them?'

He focused on a point beyond Libby's shoulder. 'This is our deal.'

'No, it's not,' she whispered. 'You said you wouldn't love me, but I always presumed you would love our child.'

'Why would you presume that?' he pushed. 'You should know better than anyone that it's not a guarantee in life.'

She flinched.

'I'm sorry,' he said, lifting a hand in the air. 'I did not mean to hurt you. Only you've told me about your mother, how she was with you...'

'And it's exactly what I don't want for my child.'

'I have no intention of treating our child like an irrelevancy,' he said. 'My priority is this family. I will keep you both safe and comfortable, I will do everything in my power to ensure you are both as happy as you can be.'

'But you won't love us,' she whispered, pushing this point because it was the beginning and end of what Libby wanted. Everything else was beside the point.

'No,' he said finally, and even though Libby had been expecting this, it was still, in many ways, the dropping of the guillotine. She took a step back, nodding distractedly, eyes stinging with unshed tears.

'And that's really what you want? You really choose this?'

His eyes met hers and for a moment she felt his anguish and pain and wanted to keep pushing, to try to find the heartbroken little boy inside of him and make everything better for that child. But then he closed himself off, visibly straightening, his features becoming taut and unyielding. 'Yes.'

'Even when I am telling you that I understand? I understand you're scared, I understand why, and I will walk every step of the way on this journey at your side, understanding that you will make mistakes, that you will need help sometimes, to really let yourself love. You're not even willing to try?'

His eyes slashed through her. 'You're wrong about me, about all of this. I hope you can accept that.'

CHAPTER FOURTEEN

SHE COULDN'T. SHE wanted to. She wanted to because she knew that loving Raul meant accepting this was his way. She couldn't change him, not if he didn't want to change, but she could prove to him that she was different to everyone else in his life, by sticking by him, even when he was doing his level best to push her away.

Wasn't that the point? He'd never had anyone actually stick with him.

He'd been passed around from foster home to foster home; he'd never been accepted and welcomed and loved. He'd learned to develop a thick skin because he'd had to, and now Libby had a chance to show him that she really was different.

But living with Raul after that conversation was a lesson in despair for Libby. She felt it every moment of every day. She was going through the motions of her life, rattling around the enormous penthouse as if in a nightmare from which she couldn't wake. He was there, yet they rarely spoke. He enquired after her health each morning, her pregnancy symptoms, but it was all so cold and businesslike, it left a yawning chasm in the centre of Libby's chest.

Raul had worked long hours before, but now he barely

seemed to sleep. When he wasn't in his office he was in the home gym, running as though a pride of lions was after him. Libby tried to keep busy with the nursery, with online birth classes, with books and movies and workouts of her own—she chose yoga stretches designed for pregnancy—but she was always aware of him. Always aware of his silence, his rejection.

She wanted to be with him, because Raul deserved that. But what about her?

Didn't she deserve better than this? Could she really live with someone who wouldn't even try to see what they shared?

On the one hand, Libby was tempted to leave. To run away and go home, tail between her legs, and work out how to do this on her own after all. But always the thought of Raul stopped her. She did love him. It was that simple. So she couldn't ignore what he needed, even when it ran contrary to her own needs. She had to stay, to show him she was willing to put her money where her mouth was. She meant what she'd said: she wasn't going anywhere because he was worth loving, even if that hurt her.

In the end, it wasn't really Libby's decision though. Four days after Libby had poured out her heart to Raul, he came into the kitchen while she was fixing a light dinner for herself. She had very little appetite but for the sake of the baby tended to have a small bowl of fruit and yoghurt for dinner.

'This can't go on.' It was hardly a promising start to the sentence.

She stopped slicing the tops off strawberries and gave him the full force of her attention.

'I've bought an apartment downstairs. I'll move out. I've organised for a nurse to come and stay in the guest room; you'll still have around-the-clock care. No climbing ladders,' he added with a tight smile. 'I'll attend medical appointments with you and, naturally, I'll be at the birth.' He cleared his throat. 'Once the baby is born, we'll work out a solution for co-parenting.'

Libby swayed a little and had to reach out and grip the counter top to stop from falling to the floor.

'Living in the same building will mean we can both be present in the baby's life. I know that's important to both of us.'

Libby's body seemed to exist in a strange half-life. She felt every organ shutting down; her blood seemed to stop pumping. Every feeling of rejection she'd known in the course of her life seemed to swirl around her all over again. She was unlovable. Unwanted.

'Oh,' was all she could say, and it emerged as a strangled, incoherent, breathy sound, garbled by a rush of grief.

Worse than loving Raul and knowing he didn't return those feelings was being pushed out of his life for good. Sidelined and having his place taken by paid-for medical staff.

Libby had known she would need to fight for this, to get through those stubbornly held barriers of his, but suddenly the fight seemed insurmountable. He had to fight too, just a little bit. Just enough to give her faith she could get through to him. How could she believe that when he was literally walking away from her?

'You're not the only one who's been let down,' she said quietly, staring at him and doing her best to keep emotion out of her voice and face. 'You're not the only one who's been hurt, rejected, who's absolutely terrified of what this might mean.'

A muscle jerked in his jaw; he stayed perfectly still.

'But I'm more afraid of losing you,' she said simply. 'I love you, and I want this family to be real.'

'That's because it's your fantasy,' he said with obvious frustration. 'You want a family so badly you've deluded yourself into seeing something that's not here.'

She drew in a sharp breath, the charge one that wounded deeply because it could well have been true. Libby knew it wasn't; she understood the accuracy of her heart's desires. But she felt that he'd taken her deepest secrets and weaponised them to win his argument.

'I won't be responsible for hurting you, Libby. That was never my intention. If I had known what marriage and children meant to you, I might not have suggested this arrangement in the first place; that was my mistake. But I can fix it.'

'By moving out?' she asked quietly.

'Yes.'

'You think that will make me stop loving you?'

'It might allow you the necessary perspective to see things as they really are.'

She let out a garbled laugh. 'That's ironic,' she muttered. 'Given you're the one who's blind to the truth, not me.'

His lips clamped together, as if physically biting back whatever he'd been about to say. 'You have my number. Call me if you need anything.'

Libby stared at him, reality sinking in. 'You're seriously leaving?'

'I'll have someone come to collect my clothes later today.'

Libby's eyes swept shut. The pain was immense, but she refused to let him see it. She was too proud, but also, she didn't want to burden him with it.

'Okay,' she said quietly, stoically. 'If that's what you want.'

'It's for the best.'

When she opened her eyes, Raul was gone.

Raul had intentionally kept his personal possessions sparse. He'd always known in the back of his mind that he would need to be ready to run at any point. If life had taught him one lesson consistently, it was the importance of that. And so he'd run.

Not far.

Just two floors down, to an apartment that was comparatively small but still boasted all of the hallmarks of opulence the building was renowned for. And here, he told himself, he'd find peace and salvation. Here, he'd start to feel like himself again, because Libby was finally away from him.

Except she wasn't.

Libby wasn't just a presence…she was an absence. He felt her even when she wasn't there.

He ached for her. Not just physically, but even the sight of her.

He'd become used to having her in his space. To knowing she was in the kitchen or the nursery, or even her bedroom. He'd found himself staring into space and

imagining her reading or watching a movie, curled up on
the sofa. Even when he'd stuck to his guns and remained
locked away in his office, she'd been a part of his day.

And she still was.

It drove him crazy, and Raul became even more determined to conquer her control over him. To run away
not just physically, but mentally too. He'd come dangerously close to forgetting how he lived his life—and
why—but he'd escaped in time. He'd run before it got
real, hadn't he?

Libby found it was far easier to give paid nursing staff the
slip than it had been Raul. For all that Raul had clearly
given instructions that Libby was to be shadowed, there
was no medical need for her to have a constant compan-
ion and she found it simple enough to step out when necessary. The solitude was her godsend.

She had found a small park a few blocks away and
she enjoyed sitting on one of the benches with a coffee
each morning, watching the parents and nannies playing with the young children, a hand on her belly as she
thought of her little one. Libby could easily imagine how
nice it would be in summer to come here with her baby,
stretch a picnic blanket out beneath a tree and enjoy the
sounds of children laughing and playing and all the good
things in life.

Except in those fantasies Libby and the baby weren't
alone.

Raul was always there, relaxing, smiling, close, doting.

A lump formed easily in Libby's throat these days;
tears were never far away. It had been two weeks since
she'd seen Raul, though he'd texted each morning to

check on her and she knew he spoke to the nurse regularly, to keep tabs on her physical health.

He was making it obvious that he cared for the baby, the pregnancy, that he was willing to look after Libby's medical needs, but that was where he drew the line.

Perhaps she'd been wrong about him?

Or maybe she'd been right, and he did love her, but he just couldn't overcome the damage wrought by his childhood and fight for what they shared. If that were the case, she had to accept it. She could love him with all her heart, but it wasn't enough for Raul. It never would be.

After an hour or so, Libby began to make her way home, pausing at a newsstand on the corner to buy a paper, then heading to the building.

'Good morning, Mrs Ortega,' the doorman, John, greeted her deferentially as she entered.

'Hello.' She smiled back.

'Must be getting close now?' He grinned, nodding towards her stomach.

She patted her round belly. 'Yes.' Even while discussing the baby, she couldn't dredge up a smile. Misery saturated Libby.

'Such lovely news.'

She nodded awkwardly, then moved inside, pressed the button and waited for the lift. When the doors opened, Raul was staring right back at her. Her heart accelerated dangerously, thudding into her throat. She simply stood and stared. The whole world seemed wonky and uneven. Everything inside Libby froze.

Two weeks.

For two weeks she had been striving to make her peace with this, to accept how much she loved and missed him and find a way to coexist with those feelings, to exist in a state of happiness regardless, but just the sight of Raul was like a punch right in her gut.

She stared at him and took a step backwards. The lift doors began to close. Raul's hand came out, keeping them open for her.

'Going up?' he asked, his voice strained even to Libby's ears.

'It's okay. I'll wait.'

'We can ride in the same elevator together, Libby, for God's sake.'

She bit down on her lip, blinking away from him. It was only the possibility of people staring, speculating, that had her taking a step inside the lift and she wished she hadn't as soon as the doors zipped closed and the air seemed to spark with awareness in a way that threatened to pull at all the threads of her sanity.

She tapped her security card to the lift console then pressed her back as hard to the wall as she could. Mercifully, the lift was swift and the doors had opened again before she knew it, onto Raul's floor, but he made no room to leave.

'This is you, isn't it?' she said woodenly.

'I'll see you home.'

She almost scoffed at the stupidity of that. As if he cared. But she wouldn't give him the satisfaction of arguing. She simply shrugged, kept staring straight ahead, and a moment later the doors pinged open once more, this time into the penthouse apartment they'd once shared.

As Libby moved to step past him, Raul put a hand out. Not to Libby, but rather to keep the doors open.

She slowed a little once in the foyer, knowing she had

to say something, to at least acknowledge and farewell. She turned, and her heart thumped.

'How are you?' he asked, the question gruff, his eyes raking over her as if the answer lay in her appearance.

'Fine,' she lied. 'And you?'

His smile was bitter. 'Also fine. But then, I am not growing a human inside of me.'

Libby lifted one shoulder. 'Half the time I forget I am. Except at night,' she added, babbling because she was nervous. 'At night, he or she is very active.'

'Are you finding it hard to sleep?'

'Yes,' she said, and she was glad that he would presume it was because of their somersaulting baby, and not the real reason: that she was tormented by thoughts and memories of Raul and what might have been, to the point she found sleep untenable. Their eyes held, yet both were silent. The atmosphere pulsated, and then Libby took a step backwards.

'Well, nice seeing you,' she said quietly. 'Take care.' And she spun away from him quickly, as though her life depended on it.

Raul rode back down to his own apartment with a scowl on his features and a strange feeling in his gut. A feeling that he was going in the opposite direction, like swimming upstream or pushing a magnet against an equal pole. It was really stupid.

He strode into his apartment, changed into his gym gear and left the building, determined to run until he understood himself once more.

Understanding didn't come. The more he ran, the less anything made sense.

Oh, he knew what he *should* want, what was right and smart and safe, but the thought of living two floors below Libby and their baby now seemed preposterous. Two weeks ago, he'd convinced himself it was the right thing for everybody, but how could that be so?

It was clearly not right for Libby—she looked exhausted and shell-shocked. She looked hurt and betrayed.

And for him?

He couldn't analyse his feelings, only he knew everything was wrong. The instincts that had kept him safe for so long, the instincts that had taught him to run at the first sign of connection, to preserve a solid amount of space around himself as though his life depended on it, were pulling him in a different direction now, making him want things that were counter to every goal he'd ever had in life.

He pulled to the edge of the sidewalk and stared across the street, closing his eyes for a moment and letting himself step fully into Libby's rosy dream for them. The family she'd described. The love. The warmth, the promise to *always* love him, no matter what. When he stepped into that vision of his future, he felt a want that was greater than any he'd ever known. For a moment, he let himself imagine it was real, that he could trust her, that Libby would protect him, that he could trust her not to hurt him, that loving her wouldn't mean one day he would have to suffer the most immense loss of his life.

But it was only a fantasy, just like he'd told her. Because at some point the dream would crack. She'd leave him, like everyone else ever had. Or worse, he'd leave her. He'd hurt her, more than he had already, and he'd never be able to forgive himself for that.

Raul began to run once more, but it didn't matter how far he went: he couldn't outrun the tortured nature of his indecision and finally, as he approached the apartment, he stopped running, not just physically, but also mentally.

Libby scared him. She always had.

Right from the beginning, when she'd been willing to put her own life on the line to save his.

But this was different.

She was offering a future that he'd never allowed himself to hope for, because he'd been trained to believe it was beyond his reach.

What if it wasn't?

What if Libby's vision for their family could be a reality? What if he'd been wrong about everything?

'I was informed it's your favourite,' Raul said, holding up a bag of take-out from the Chinese restaurant a few blocks away.

Libby eyed it suspiciously. 'Informed by whom?'

'That would be me.' Her nurse, Veronica, smiled as she pulled her handbag over one shoulder. 'I'll see you tomorrow.'

Libby frowned. 'You're leaving?'

'Call if you need anything,' Veronica said with a nod and wave, disappearing into the lift. Libby watched her go, perplexed.

'Raul, what's going on?'

The smell of the Chinese was wafting towards Libby and her tummy groaned with hunger. She ignored it.

'Can we have dinner? We should talk.'

Libby stared at him, her gut rolling, tightening, confusion making her insides hurt. 'I—' She stared at him, wanting to tell him no. But hadn't she promised that she would love him always? That she would be there for him? While her self-defence mechanism was to push him away now, before he could push her any further, that wasn't right. She needed to *show* him that she loved him, no matter what, not just say it.

'Okay.' She tried to keep her voice neutral. 'Dinner,' she added, as a midway point to looking after herself too.

His eyes showed relief and one corner of his lip lifted in a tight half-smile. 'Thank you.'

His gratitude was unexpected.

Libby busied herself removing plates and water glasses from the kitchen and laying out the table, while Raul removed the lids from the meals and set them up between their two seats. He'd ordered her favourites—she had to credit Veronica for that intel too.

'So,' Libby said, taking a seat opposite Raul, hands folded neatly in her lap, 'what do we need to talk about?'

'The other day...' he said, eyes meeting hers then glancing away.

She frowned. 'What other day?'

'Here, in the kitchen. The conversation we had.'

'That was weeks ago,' she muttered, colouring.

'I'm aware of that.'

'It's just, when you said "the other day" I thought you meant a few days ago, not...' Her voice trailed off.

How could she tell him that a few weeks ago felt like an eternity to her because she'd missed him so damned much? He must know she felt that way, but Libby didn't need to bang him over the head with the truth of that.

'Anyway,' she finished unevenly, 'what do you want to discuss?'

'I think I made a mistake.'

Libby's gut churned; she refused to let hope into the cracks of her heart. Carefully, staying very still, she said, 'Oh?'

Raul's Adam's apple shifted beneath his stubble. His features bore their trademark mask of arrogant control but Libby saw through it. Regardless of her best intentions, hope burst through her.

'Raul,' she murmured. 'What are you trying to say?'

'I don't want to live apart from you.' His brow furrowed, as he concentrated harder. 'I want to live with you.'

For her own sake, Libby had to take this slowly, and also be very specific about what he was saying. This was not a time to rush to conclusions because she *wanted* him to want the same things she did.

'You mean, how we were before? You want it to go back to the way it was before that morning?'

'Yes,' he said with a smile, then shook his head. 'No.' He dragged a hand through his hair. 'I am terrible at this.'

Libby waited patiently.

'I want to live with you, properly. As husband and wife.'

Beneath the table, Libby fidgeted her hands in her lap. It was so close to what she wanted, but still she was careful, cautious, measured.

'Why?' she asked simply, because there could be a dozen reasons for his change of heart. Worry about her health, protectiveness of the baby, a pragmatic preference to be near to one another for the late stages of the pregnancy. None of which equated to the happy-ever-after Libby wanted.

'Why do you think?'

'I don't know, and it's important to understand exactly what you're saying,' she murmured. 'I need to manage my own expectations for this.'

'I think you might be right,' he said slowly, carefully.

Simply for something to do, Libby reached out and took an egg roll, placed it on her plate but then just stared at it.

'I think there might be something fated about our meeting.'

Her heart leaped into her throat.

'Let me show you something,' he said quietly, reaching into his pocket and removing a necklace—a chain with a simple pendant on it. He stared at it a moment, his expression impossible to interpret. 'It's the only thing of my parents' that I possess. It was my mother's. I don't remember her, or him. As I told you, they died when I was very young. This is all I was left.' He moved it from one hand to the other, then handed it over to Libby.

She turned it over to see cursive script on the back, in Spanish. 'What does it say?'

'It's a translation of an old English poem, about the value of living every moment of every day, the importance of not letting opportunities pass one by.'

Libby read the Spanish words but heard Raul's translation, then passed the necklace back to him, still doing her best to be guarded with her heart, even when she was starting to hope against hope that her wildest dreams were coming true.

'You were right about me,' he said. 'About my childhood, about how it shaped me. I was made to feel worthless by everyone in my life until I met Maria and Pedro, and even them I kept at arm's length. Every relationship in my life is transactional. I don't have friendships that are more than skin-deep. I am careful not to get close to anyone. And with you, it felt even more imperative to maintain those boundaries because, from the very first meeting, I knew on some level that you were a threat to how I live my life. That you could break down my boundaries if you tried to. I have done my best to control this, but I can't.'

Libby's eyes stung.

'I told myself I walked away from this to protect you, but the truth is, I wanted to protect myself. You were offering me your love, something I wanted so fiercely that I knew if anything happened, and you stopped loving me, it would be the worst pain I'd ever known. I have never wanted anything like I have this.' He waved a hand around the apartment.

'So you left.'

'But it was too late,' he said. 'The damage is done. You love me, and that means something.'

'It doesn't have to,' she whispered, not wanting him to come back because he pitied her or was grateful to her.

'It means *everything*,' he clarified. 'Even if it is only for now, even if this is temporary, I have to be here, to live this with you. I have to love you back, because I've come to realise there is no alternative. Real love cannot be controlled, as it turns out, no matter how determined you are.'

Libby's heart soared now, given freedom by the hope she'd finally allowed to rein in her body.

'Yes,' she whispered, though what question she was

answering she couldn't say. But somehow she needed him to know she agreed, she approved, that she understood.

His eyes scanned her face. 'I'm not going to be good at this.'

Libby's laugh was tremulous as she stood, coming around the table and moving to sit in Raul's lap. 'I can live with that.'

'I do love you,' he said. 'I cannot let you—this opportunity I have somehow been given—slip through my fingers. You are my fate, my all.' He stared at her, then shrugged. 'I just… love you.'

'I thought so.' She smiled serenely.

'How on earth could you have that kind of faith in me?'

She pressed her forehead to his. 'I knew you loved me, Raul. I just didn't know if you'd be brave enough to admit it to yourself.'

His hand ran lightly over her spine. 'I hope I can one day be worthy of the faith you had in me.'

She pressed her lips to his. 'You already are.'

EPILOGUE

IF RAUL HAD any lingering doubts about the strength of his love for Libby—and there were none—those doubts would have disappeared entirely in the face of her heroism and courage whilst delivering their baby.

It was not an easy delivery. There were many times when Raul thought he would undo every blissful moment of life with Libby if he could only go back in time and not sleep with her that fateful afternoon, if it meant she could be spared this pain and torment.

For twenty hours she laboured, and he was with her every step of the way until finally, in the small hours of the morning, their baby was delivered and Raul knew, the moment he looked at their daughter, that his heart—what small piece he had kept of it after meeting Libby—was no longer, and never would be, his own. He was beholden to these two women now, utterly and completely. They were his reason for living, his purpose, his life, come what may.

Libby was serene in the hour after birth, her eyes fluttering closed, a beatific smile on her face as she held their daughter cradled to her chest, Raul perching on the edge of the bed. This was his family; it was where he belonged.

* * *

Life was never the same after that. Raul and Libby had both been shaped by their experiences, and had developed skills to help them cope with life. Separate, they had existed and they had been okay, but together they really, truly lived. Success took on a different metric for Raul now—if Libby and baby Maria were happy, he was happy.

They lived as the three of them for a single year before Libby was once more pregnant, this time with twin boys, and a year after that another little girl joined their family. Raul had gone from intending to live a solitary life, completely his own person, to finding that his heart simply grew and grew with every new addition to their family—including, to his surprise, the Retriever they adopted when their youngest child was two years old.

They didn't stay in the penthouse apartment for long. One day, while pregnant with the twins, on a drive through the Hamptons, they pulled over to have a picnic on the beach and happened to find a spot right near a big old home that just exuded happiness. From the timber walls to the old tin roof, wraparound balcony and wide steps that led to a porch swing, the house was everything Libby had ever dreamed of. Even the garden seemed to conspire to seduce Libby—huge geranium and lavender bushes lined the gravelled front path, reminding her forcefully of the flowers of home.

'Oh, Raul,' she said, leaning her head against his chest. 'Isn't it the most beautiful thing you've ever seen?'

Raul took one look at Libby's face and knew he would move heaven and earth to gift her this house just as soon as he could. It did not take heaven and earth, just an offer to the owners that was a fair bit above market value, but in Raul's eyes it was worth every penny for the surprise of being able to drive Libby back the following weekend, this time with the keys in his possession.

She wept with happiness, and Raul grinned. He had wanted to give Libby the world, and this sweet old beach house seemed like as good a place to start as any.

For Libby, the house became a home the moment they crossed the threshold. It was everything she'd always dreamed of. Pretty without being fancy, welcoming and comfortable, the sort of place she could raise her kids away from the opulence and wealth of Raul's world—not that he went in for any of that stuff, anyway. He was finally delegating to his more than qualified executives, accepting that he could zoom out his focus from his business interests and still ensure the ongoing success of his company. Taking a step back from his role had opened the door for new opportunities anyway: he had begun to invest in worthy start-ups, supporting people with big ideas and a lack of resourcing, in the hope that he could do for them what Maria and Pedro's support had done for him.

And then there was Libby, for whom Raul was the biggest champion.

While she was happier than she could express raising their children and being married to Raul, he knew and understood that she had so many skills beyond these, and he never missed an opportunity to remind her she could do whatever she wanted. He would care for the children, he would be whatever she needed, so she could pursue her own ambitions, to really live up to her potential.

It wasn't until their youngest started school that she finally felt ready to turn her focus to something else. Gone was the desire to pursue anything related to book-keeping, which she'd considered out of desperation what felt like a lifetime ago. That would have been a career of practicality, to enable her to work from home and care for Maria—way back when she thought she would be doing it all alone. Now, she wasn't alone. She was supported and cherished beyond belief, and in the years since marrying Raul she had come to realise there was one passion she couldn't ignore. Another hand of fate?

Libby enrolled in a course to study jewellery making. 'It's not just the jewellery,' she explained to Raul enthusiastically as she came close to finishing the course. 'It's what it means. It's the idea that each piece becomes a keepsake, something special and meaningful that can evoke emotions all over again. Every time I look at my ring, I think of you,' she said. 'And your mother's necklace keeps her with you,' she said gently, eyes on his face. 'It matters.'

'Yes, Libby, it does,' he agreed, and he kissed her because it was the only way he could think of to express his absolute, all-consuming love for his wife.

Every now and again, Raul found himself imagining 'What if?' What if he hadn't gone to Sydney that weekend? What if Libby hadn't been sent to the boat? What if those teenagers hadn't attempted to steal it? What if he hadn't finally forced himself to understand what he felt for her, what he wanted from her? What if he'd actually been stupid enough to let her go? But then he looked at Libby and she smiled, and he relaxed, because fate had always been driving them to this—Raul was simply along for the ride, and it was a ride he intended to enjoy to its fullest for the rest of his life on earth.

* * * * *

Were you swept off your feet by
Pregnant Before the Proposal?

Then don't miss these other stories
by Clare Connelly!

The Boss's Forbidden Assistant
Twelve Nights in the Prince's Bed
The Sicilian's Deal For "I Do"
Contracted and Claimed by the Boss
His Runaway Royal

Available now!

HARLEQUIN

Reader Service

Enjoyed your book?

Try the perfect subscription for Romance readers and get more great books like this delivered right to your door.

See why over 10+ million readers have tried Harlequin Reader Service.

Start with a Free Welcome Collection with free books and a gift—valued over $20.

Choose any series in print or ebook. See website for details and order today:

TryReaderService.com/subscriptions